Franz Kafka

The Metamorphosis, A Hunger Artist, In the Penal Colony, and Other Stories

Translated
by
Ian Johnston
Vancouver Island University
Nanaimo, British Columbia
Canada

Richer Resources Publications
Arlington, Virginia
USA

Kafka
Metamorphosis, A Hunger Artist, In the Penal Colony, and Other
Stories

Second Edition (2011)

Richer Resources Publications
1926 N. Woodrow Street
Arlington, Virginia 22207
USA

or to our website at www.RicherResourcesPublications.com

ISBN 978-1-935238-82-9
LCCN 2009936926

Published by Richer Resources Publications, Arlington, VA
Printed in the United States of America

For Kimberley

INTRODUCTORY NOTE

Franz Kafka (1883-1924) was born in Prague, now in the Czech Republic, but at that time part of the Austro-Hungarian Empire, to a middle-class Jewish, German-speaking family. For most of his working life he was employed as an insurance official. He published a number of stories in German, mainly in literary magazines and journals, but was little known during his lifetime. He instructed his literary executor to destroy all his manuscripts, a final request which the executor refused to carry out.

Kafka was sick much of his life with various illnesses, the most serious of which was tuberculosis, from which he died in 1924. After his death, his reputation gradually improved, and Kafka is now recognized as one of the greatest writers of modernist European fiction. Kafka is buried in Prague.

The second edition of this collection of Kafka stories is the same as the first, except for some corrections and minor changes to the text and the formatting.

TABLE OF CONTENTS

BEFORE THE LAW[1]

Before the law sits a gatekeeper. To this gatekeeper comes a man from the country who asks to gain entry into the law. But the gatekeeper says that he cannot grant him entry at the moment. The man thinks about it and then asks if he will be allowed to come in sometime later on. "It is possible," says the gatekeeper, "but not now." The gate to the law stands open, as always, and the gatekeeper walks to the side, so the man bends over in order to see through the gate into the inside. When the gatekeeper notices that, he laughs and says: "If it tempts you so much, try going inside in spite of my prohibition. But take note. I am powerful. And I am only the most lowly gatekeeper. But from room to room stand gatekeepers, each more powerful than the other. I cannot endure even one glimpse of the third." The man from the country has not expected such difficulties: the law should always be accessible for everyone, he thinks, but as he now looks more closely at the gatekeeper in his fur coat, at his large pointed nose and his long, thin, black Tartar's beard, he decides that it would be better to wait until he gets permission to go inside. The gatekeeper gives him a stool and allows him to sit down at the side in front of the gate. There he sits for days and years. He makes many attempts to be let in, and he wears the gatekeeper out with his requests. The gatekeeper often interrogates him briefly, questioning him about his homeland and many other things, but they are indifferent questions, the kind great men put, and at the end he always tells him once more that he cannot let him inside yet. The man, who has equipped himself with many things for his journey, spends everything, no matter how valuable, to win over the gatekeeper. The latter takes it all but, as he does so, says, "I am taking this only so that you do not think you have failed to do anything." During the many years the man observes the gatekeeper almost continuously. He forgets the other gatekeepers, and this first one seems to him the only obstacle for entry into the law. He curses the unlucky circumstance, in the first years thoughtlessly and out loud; later, as he grows old, he only mumbles to himself. He

---

[1]First published in *Die Selbstwehr*, September 1915. The story also appears in Kafka's novel *The Trial*, which was not published until after his death.

becomes childish and, since in the long years studying the gate-keeper he has also come to know the fleas in his fur collar, he even asks the fleas to help him persuade the gatekeeper. Finally his eyesight grows weak, and he does not know whether things are really darker around him or whether his eyes are merely deceiving him. But he recognizes now in the darkness an illumi-nation which breaks inextinguishably out of the gateway to the law. Now he no longer has much time to live. Before his death he gathers in his head all his experiences of the entire time up into one question which he has not yet put to the gatekeeper. He waves to him, since he can no longer lift up his stiffening body. The gatekeeper has to bend way down to him, for the great differ-ence has changed things considerably to the disadvantage of the man. "What do you still want to know now?" asks the gatekeeper. "You are insatiable." "Everyone strives after the law," says the man, "so how is it that in these many years no one except me has requested entry?" The gatekeeper sees that the man is already dying and, in order to reach his diminishing sense of hearing, he shouts at him, "Here no one else can gain entry, since this ent-rance was assigned only to you. I'm going now to close it."

UP IN THE GALLERY[1]

If some frail tubercular lady circus rider were to be driven in circles around and around the arena for months and months without interruption in front of a tireless public on a swaying horse by a merciless whip-wielding master of ceremonies, spinning on the horse, throwing kisses and swaying at the waist, and if this performance, amid the incessant roar of the orchestra and the ventilators, were to continue into the ever-expanding, grey future, accompanied by applause, which died down and then swelled up again, from hands which were really steam hammers, perhaps then a young visitor to the gallery might rush down the long staircase through all the levels, burst into the ring, and cry "Stop!" through the fanfares of the constantly adjusting orchestra.

But since things are not like that—since a beautiful lady, in white and red, flies in through curtains which proud men in livery open in front of her, since the director, with the devotion of an animal, seeks her eyes, breathes in her direction, and, as a precaution, lifts her up on the dapple-grey horse, as if she were his granddaughter, the one he loved more than anything else, as she starts a dangerous journey, but he cannot decide to give the signal with his whip and finally, controlling himself, gives it a crack, runs right beside the horse with his mouth open, follows the rider's leaps with a sharp gaze, hardly capable of comprehending her skill, tries to warn her by calling out in English, furiously castigating the grooms holding hoops, telling them to pay the most scrupulous attention, and begs the orchestra, with upraised arms, to be quiet before the great somersault, finally lifts the small woman down from the trembling horse, kisses her on both cheeks, and considers no public tribute adequate, while she herself, supported by him, high on the tips of her toes, with dust swirling around her, arms outstretched and little head thrown back, wants to share her luck with the entire circus—since this is how things are, the visitor to the gallery puts his face on the railing and, sinking into the final march as if into a difficult dream, weeps, without realizing it.

[1]First published in the collection of stories *A Country Doctor*, 1919.

AN IMPERIAL MESSAGE[1]

The Emperor—so they say—has sent a message, directly from his deathbed, to you alone, his pathetic subject, a tiny shadow which has taken refuge at the furthest distance from the imperial sun. He ordered the herald to kneel down beside his death bed and whispered the message to him. He thought it was so important that he had the herald repeat it back to him. He confirmed the accuracy of the verbal message by nodding his head. And in front of the entire crowd of those who have come to witness his death —all the obstructing walls have been broken down and all the great ones of his empire are standing in a circle on the broad and high soaring flights of stairs—in front of all of them he dispatched his herald. The messenger started off at once, a powerful, tireless man. Sticking one arm out and then another, he makes his way through the crowd. If he runs into resistance, he points to his breast where there is a sign of the sun. So he moves forward easily, unlike anyone else. But the crowd is so huge; its dwelling places are infinite. If there were an open field, how he would fly along, and soon you would hear the marvellous pounding of his fist on your door. But instead of that, how futile are all his efforts. He is still forcing his way through the private rooms of the innermost palace. He will never win his way through. And if he did manage that, nothing would have been achieved. He would have to fight his way down the steps, and, if he managed to do that, nothing would have been achieved. He would have to stride through the courtyards, and after the courtyards the second palace encircling the first, and, then again, stairs and courtyards, and then, once again, a palace, and so on for thousands of years. And if he finally did burst through the outermost door—but that can never, never happen—the royal capital city, the centre of the world, is still there in front of him, piled high and full of sediment. No one pushes his way through here, certainly not with a message from a dead man. But you sit at your window and dream to yourself of that message when evening comes.

[1]First published in *Die Selbstwehr*, 1919. The passage is also part of the longer story "The Great Wall of China."

JACKALS AND ARABS[1]

We were camping in the oasis. My companions were asleep. An Arab, tall and white, went past me. He had been tending to his camels and was going to his sleeping place.

I threw myself on my back into the grass. I wanted to sleep. I couldn't. The howling of a jackal in the distance—I sat up straight again. And what had been so far away was suddenly close by. A swarming pack of jackals around me, their eyes flashing dull gold and going out, slender bodies moving in a quick, coordinated manner, as if they were being controlled by a whip.

One of them came from behind, pushed himself under my arm, right against me, as if it needed my warmth, then stepped in front of me and spoke, almost eye to eye with me.

"I'm the oldest jackal for miles around. I'm happy I'm still able to welcome you here. I had already almost given up hope, for we've been waiting for you an infinitely long time. My mother waited, and her mother, and all her mothers, right back to the mother of all jackals. Believe me!"

"That surprises me," I said, forgetting to light the pile of wood which lay ready to keep the jackals away with its smoke, "I'm very surprised to hear that. I've come from the high north merely by chance and am in the middle of a short trip. What do you want then, Jackal?"

As if encouraged by this conversation, which was perhaps far too friendly, they drew their circle more closely around me, all panting and snarling.

"We know," the oldest began, "that you come from the north. Our hope rests on that very point. In the north there is a way of understanding things which one cannot find here among the Arabs. You know, from their cool arrogance one cannot strike a spark of common sense. They kill animals to eat them, and they disregard rotting carcasses."

[1]First published in *Der Jude*, October 1917.

"Don't speak so loud," I said. "There are Arabs sleeping close by."

"You really are a stranger," said the jackal. "Otherwise you would know that throughout the history of the world a jackal has never yet feared an Arab. Should we fear them? Is it not misfortune enough that we have been cast out among such people?"

"Maybe—that could be," I said. "I'm not up to judging things which are so far removed from me. It seems to be a very old conflict—it's probably in the blood and so perhaps will only end with blood."

"You are very clever" said the old jackal, and they all panted even more quickly, their lungs breathing rapidly, although they were standing still. A bitter smell streamed out of their open jaws—at times I could tolerate it only by clenching my teeth. "You are very clever. What you said corresponds to our ancient doctrine. So we take their blood, and the quarrel is over."

"Oh!" I said, more sharply than I intended, "they'll defend themselves. They'll shoot you down in droves with their guns."

"You do not understand us," he said, "a characteristic of human beings which has not disappeared, not even in the high north. We are not going to kill them. The Nile would not have enough water to wash us clean. The mere sight of their living bodies makes us run away immediately into cleaner air, into the desert, which, for that very reason, is our home."

All the jackals surrounding us—and in the meantime even more had come up from a distance—lowered their heads between their front legs and cleaned them with their paws. It was as if they wanted to conceal an aversion which was so terrible, that I would have much preferred to take a big jump and escape beyond their circle.

"So what do you intend to do," I asked. I wanted to stand up, but I couldn't. Two young animals were holding me firmly from behind with their jaws biting into my jacket and shirt. I had to remain sitting. "They are holding your train," said the old jackal seriously, by way of explanation, "a mark of respect." "They should let me go," I cried out, turning back and forth between the old one and the young ones. "Of course, they will," said the old one, "if that's what you want. But it will take a little while, for, as is our habit, they have dug their teeth in deep and must first let their jaws open gradually. Meanwhile, listen to our request." "Your conduct has not made me particularly receptive to it," I said. "Don't make us pay for our clumsiness," he said, and now for the first time he brought the plaintive tone of his natural voice to his assistance. "We are poor animals—all we have is our teeth. For everything we want to do—good and bad—the only thing available to us is our teeth." "So what do you want?" I asked, only slightly reassured.

"Sir," he cried out, and all the jackals howled. To me it sounded very remotely like a melody. "Sir, you should end the quarrel which divides the world in two. Our ancestors described a man like you as the one who will do it. We must be free of the Arabs— with air we can breathe, a view of the horizon around us clear of Arabs, no cries of pain from a sheep which an Arab has knifed, and every animal should die peacefully and be left undisturbed for us to drain it empty and clean it right down to the bones. Cleanliness—that's what we want—nothing but cleanliness." Now they were all crying and sobbing. "How can you bear it in this world, you noble heart and sweet entrails? Dirt is their white; dirt is their black; their beards are horrible; looking at the corner of their eyes makes one spit; and if they lift their arms, hell opens up in their arm pits. And that's why, sir, that's why, my dear sir, with the help of your all-capable hands, with the help of your all-capable hands you must use these scissors to slit right through their throats." He jerked his head, and in response a jackal came up carrying on its canine tooth a small pair of sewing scissors covered with old rust.

"So finally the scissors—it's time to stop!" cried the Arab leader of our caravan, who had crept up on us from downwind. Now he swung his gigantic whip.

The jackals all fled quickly, but still remained at some distance huddled closely together, many animals so close and tense that it looked as if they were in a narrow pen with jack o' lanterns flying around them.

"So, you too, sir, have seen and heard this spectacle," said the Arab, laughing as cheerfully as the reticence of his race permitted. "So you know what the animals want," I asked. "Of course, sir," he said. "That's common knowledge—as long as there are Arabs, these scissors wander through the deserts and will wander with us until the end of days. Every European is offered them for the great work; every European is exactly the one who seems to them qualified to do it. These animals have an absurd hope. They're idiots, real idiots. That's why we're fond of them. They are our dogs, finer than the ones you have. Now, watch this. In the night a camel died. I have had it brought here."

Four bearers came and threw the heavy carcass right in front of us. No sooner was it lying there than the jackals raised their voices. Every one of them crept forward, its body scraping the ground, as if drawn by an irresistible rope. They had forgotten the Arabs, forgotten their hatred. The presence of a powerfully stinking dead body wiped out everything and enchanted them. One of them was already hanging at the camel's throat and with its first bite had found the artery. Like a small raging pump which—with a determination matched only by its hopelessness—seeks to put out an overpowering fire, every muscle of its body pulled and twitched in its place. Then right away all of them were lying there on the corpse in a mountainous heap, working in the same way.

Then the leader cracked his sharp whip powerfully all around above them. They raised their heads, half fainting in their intoxicated state, looked at the Arab standing in front of them, started to feel the whip now hitting their muzzles, jumped away, and ran back a distance. But the camel's blood was already lying there in pools, stinking to heaven, and the body was torn wide open in several places. They could not resist. They were there again. The leader once more raised his whip. I grabbed his arm. "Sir, you are right," he said. "We'll leave them to their calling. Besides, it's time to break camp. You've seen them. Wonderful creatures, aren't they? And how they hate us!"

THE JUDGMENT[1]
for Miss Felice B.

It was a Sunday morning at the most beautiful time in spring. George Bendemann, a young merchant, was sitting in his private room on the first floor of one of the low, poorly constructed houses extending in a long row along the river, almost indistinguishable from each other except for their height and colour. He had just finished a letter to a friend from his youth who was now abroad, had sealed it in a playful and desultory manner, and now was looking, elbows propped on the writing table, out of the window at the river, the bridge, and the hills on the other shore with their delicate greenery.

He was thinking about how this friend, dissatisfied with his progress at home, had actually run off to Russia some years before. Now he ran a business in St. Petersburg, which had gotten off to a very good start but which for a long time now had appeared to be faltering, as his friend complained on his increasingly rare visits. So he was wearing himself out working to no purpose in a foreign land. The exotic full beard only poorly concealed the face George had known so well since his childhood years, and the yellowish colour of his skin seemed to indicate a developing sickness. As he explained it, he had no real connection to the colony of his countrymen in the place and also hardly any social interaction with local families and thus was resigning himself to being a permanent bachelor.

What should one write to such a man, who had obviously gone off course, a man one could feel sorry for but could not help. Should one perhaps advise him to come back home again, shift his life back here, take up once more all the old friendly relationships—there was certainly nothing to prevent that—and in addition rely on the help of friends? But at the same time that amounted to saying to him—and the more gently one said it, the more wounding it would also be—that his previous attempts had been

[1]First published in *Arkadia* in 1913.

unsuccessful, that he should finally give them up, that he must come back and allow everyone to look at him as an eternal returned prodigal, that only his friends understood anything, and that he would be an over-age child, who should simply obey his successful friends who had stayed home. And then was it even certain that all the misery one would have to put him through had a point? Perhaps it would not even succeed in bringing him back home at all—in fact, he said himself that he no longer understood conditions in his homeland—so then he would remain in his foreign country in spite of everything, embittered by the advice and even a little more estranged from his friends. But if he really followed the advice and became depressed here—not intentionally, of course, but because of his circumstances—could not cope with life, with his friends or without them, felt ashamed, and had, in fact, no homeland and no friends any more, was it not much better for him to remain abroad, just as he was? Given these facts, could one think that he would really advance himself here?

For these reasons, if one still wanted to maintain some sort of relationship by correspondence, one could not provide any real news, the way one would without any inhibitions to the most casual acquaintance. It was already more than three years since his friend had been home, and he explained this with the very inadequate excuse of the uncertainty of the political conditions in Russia, which would not allow even the briefest absence of a small businessman, while it permitted hundreds of thousands of Russians to travel around peacefully in the world. But in the course of these three years much had changed for George. Since his mother's death, which had taken place about two years earlier, George had lived with his old father in a household they shared. His friend had naturally learned about it and had expressed his sympathy in a letter with such a dry tone that the reason could only have been that the sadness of such an event is completely inconceivable in a foreign country. But since that time George had tackled both his business dealings and everything else with greater determination. Perhaps while his mother was still alive, his father's unwillingness to accept anyone else's point of view in the business had prevented George from developing a real project of his own; perhaps his father, since his mother's death, had grown slacker, although he still worked all the time in the business; perhaps fortunate circumstances had played a much more important role—something which was, in fact, highly likely—but in any case in these two years the business had developed very unexpectedly. They had had to double the staff, the cash turnover had increased fivefold, and there was no doubt that further progress lay ahead.

His friend, however, had no idea of these changes. Earlier, perhaps for the last time in that letter of condolence, he had wanted to persuade George to emigrate to Russia and had expanded upon the prospects which existed in St. Petersburg for George's particular line of business. The figures were minute compared to the scale which George's business had now acquired. But George had had no desire to write to his friend about his commercial success, and if he were to do it belatedly now, it would have looked really odd.

So George limited himself to writing to his friend only about insignificant details, the kind which pile up at random in one's memory when one is thinking things over on a peaceful Sunday. The only thing he wanted was to leave undisturbed the picture which his friend must have created of his home town during the long interval and which he would have learned to live with. And so it happened that George had announced three times to his friend in fairly widely spaced letters the engagement of an unimportant man to an equally unimportant young woman, until, quite contrary to George's intentions, the friend really began to get interested in this curious event.

But George preferred to write to him about such things rather than to confess that he himself had become engaged a month ago to a Miss Frieda Brandenfeld, a young woman from a prosperous family. He often spoke to his fiancée about this friend and about the unusual relationship he had with him in their correspondence. "Then there's no chance he'll be coming to our wedding," she said, "and yet I have the right to meet all your friends." "I don't want to upset him," George replied. "Don't misunderstand me. He would probably come, at least I think so, but he would feel compelled and hurt and would perhaps envy me—he'd certainly feel unhappy and incapable of ever coping with his unhappiness and would travel back alone. Alone—do you know what that means?" "Yes, but can't he find out about our wedding in some other way?" "That's true, but I can't prevent that. However, given his lifestyle it's unlikely." "If you have friends like that, George, you shouldn't have gotten engaged at all." "Well, we're both to blame for that, but now I wouldn't want things to be any different." And then when she, breathing rapidly under his kisses, kept insisting "Still, it truly does upset me," he really thought it would be harmless to write everything to his friend. "That's what I am, and that's just how he'll have to accept me," he said to himself. "I can't carve out of myself another man who might perhaps be more suitable for a friendship with him than I am."

And, in fact, he did inform his friend about the engagement which had taken place in the long letter which he had written that Sunday morning, in the following words "The best piece of news I have saved until the end. I have become engaged to a Miss Frieda Brandenfeld, a young woman from a well-to-do family, who first settled here long after your departure and thus whom you could hardly know. There will still be an opportunity to tell you more detailed information about my fiancée. Today it's enough for you to know that I am truly fortunate and that, as far as our mutual relationship is concerned, the only thing that has changed is that in me you will now have, instead of a completely ordinary friend, a happy friend. Moreover, in my fiancée, who sends you her warm greetings and will soon write to you herself, you acquire a sincere female friend, something which is not entirely without significance for a bachelor. I know that there are many things hindering you from coming back to visit us, but wouldn't my wedding be exactly the right opportunity to throw aside all obstacles for once? But whatever the case, do only what seems good to you, without concerning yourself about anything."

George sat for a long time at his writing table with his letter in his hand, his face turned towards the window. He barely acknowledged with an absent-minded smile someone he knew who greeted him from the lane as he walked past.

Finally he put the letter in his pocket and went out of his room, angling across a small passageway into his father's room, which he had not been in for months. There was really no need to do that, since he was always dealing with his father at work and they took their noon meal at the same time in a restaurant. In the evenings, of course, they each did as they wished, but for the most part, unless George was with friends, as was most frequently the case, or was now visiting his fiancée, they still sat for a little while, each with his own newspaper, in the living room they shared.

George was surprised how dark his father's room was, even on this sunny morning. So that was the kind of shadow cast by the high wall which rose on the other side of the narrow courtyard. His father was sitting by the window in a corner decorated with various reminders of his late lamented mother and was reading a newspaper, which he held in front of his eyes to one side, attempting in this way to compensate for some weakness in his vision. On the table stood the remains of his breakfast, not much of which appeared to have been eaten.

"Ah, George," said his father, coming up at once to meet him. His heavy night shirt opened up as he moved and the ends of it flapped around him. "My father is still a giant," said George to himself.

Then he spoke up: "It's unbearably dark in here."

"Yes, it certainly is dark," his father answered.

"And you've shut the window as well?"

"I prefer it that way."

"Well, it is quite warm outside," said George, as if continuing what he'd said earlier, and sat down.

His father cleared off the breakfast dishes and put them on a chest.

"I really only wanted to tell you," continued George, who was following the movements of the old man quite absentmindedly, "that I've now sent a report of my engagement to St. Petersburg." He pulled the letter a little way out of his pocket and let it drop back again.

"To St. Petersburg?" his father asked.

"To my friend," said George, trying to look his father in the eye. "In business he's completely different," he thought. "How sturdily he sits here with his arms folded across his chest."

"Ah yes, to your friend," said his father, with emphasis.

"Well, father, you know at first I wanted to keep quiet to him about my engagement. Out of consideration, for no other reason. You yourself know he's a difficult person. I said to myself he could well learn about my engagement from some other quarter, even if his solitary way of life makes that hardly likely—I can't prevent that—but he should never learn about it from me personally."

"And now you have been thinking about it differently?" the father asked. He set the large newspaper on the window sill and on top the newspaper his glasses, which he covered with his hand.

"Yes, now I've been reconsidering it. If he's a good friend of mine, I said to myself, then a happy engagement for me is also something fortunate for him. And so I no longer hesitated to announce it to him. But before I send the letter, I wanted to tell you about it."

"George," said his father, pulling his toothless mouth wide open, "listen to me! You've come to me about this matter, to discuss it with me. No doubt that's a credit to you. But it's nothing, worse than nothing, if you don't now tell me the complete truth. I don't want to stir up things which are not appropriate here. Since the death of our dear mother certain nasty things have been going on. Perhaps the time to talk about them has come and perhaps sooner than we think. In the business, a good deal escapes me. Perhaps it's not hidden from me—at the moment I'm not claiming it's done behind my back—I am no longer strong enough, my memory is deteriorating, I can't keep an eye on so many things any more. First of all, that's nature taking its course, and secondly the death of our dear mother was a much bigger blow to me than to you. But since we're on the subject of this letter, I beg you, George, don't deceive me. It's a trivial thing, not worth mentioning. So don't deceive me. Do you really have this friend in St. Petersburg?"

George stood up in embarrassment. "Let's forget about my friend. A thousand friends wouldn't replace my father for me. Do you know what I think? You're not taking enough care of yourself. But old age demands its due. You are indispensable to me in the business—you're very well aware of that—but if the business is going to threaten your health, I'll close it tomorrow for good. That won't happen. We must set up another life style for you. But something completely different. You sit here in the dark, and in the living room you'd have good light. You nibble at your breakfast, instead of maintaining your strength properly. You sit by the closed window, and the air would do you so much good. No, my father! I'll bring in the doctor, and we'll follow his instructions. We'll change the room. You'll move into the front room. I'll come in here. For you there won't be any change. Everything will be moved over with you. But there's time for all that. Now I'll set you in bed for a little while. You need complete rest. Come, I'll help you get undressed. You'll see. I can do it. Or do you want to go into the front room right away. Then you can lie down in my bed for now. That would make a lot of sense."

George stood close beside his father, who had let his head with its tousled white hair sink onto his chest.

"George," said his father faintly, without moving.

George knelt down immediately alongside his father. He saw the enormous pupils in his father's tired face staring right at him from the corners of his eyes.

"You don't have a friend in St. Petersburg. You have always been a jokester and even with me you've not controlled yourself. So how could you have a friend there! I simply can't believe that."

"Think about it for a moment, father," said George. He raised his father from the arm chair and took off his nightgown as he just stood there very weakly. "It will soon be almost three years since my friend visited us. I still remember that you did not particularly like him. At least twice I kept him away from you, although he was sitting right in my room. It's true I could understand your aversion to him quite well. My friend does have his peculiarities. But then you later had a really good conversation with him yourself. At the time I was so proud of the fact that you listened to him, nodded your head, and asked questions. If you think about it, you must remember. That's when he told us incredible stories about the Russian Revolution. For example, on a business trip in Kiev during a riot he saw a priest on a balcony who cut a wide bloody cross into the palm of his hand, raised his hand, and appealed to the mob. You've even repeated this story yourself now and then."

Meanwhile, George had succeeded in setting his father down again and carefully taking off the cotton trousers which he wore over his linen underwear, as well as his socks. Looking at the undergarments, which were not particularly clean, he reproached himself for having neglected his father. It certainly should have been his responsibility to look after his father's laundry. He had not yet talked explicitly with his fiancée about how they wished to make arrangements for his father's future, for they had tacitly assumed that his father would remain living alone in the old apartment. But now he quickly came to the firm decision to take his father with him into his future household. When one looked more closely, it almost seemed that the care which he was ready to provide for his father there could come too late.

He carried his father to bed in his arms. He experienced a dreadful feeling when he noticed, as he took a couple of paces to the bed, that his father was playing with the watch chain on his chest. He could not put him in the bed right away, so firm was his father's grip on this watch chain.

But as soon as he was in bed, all seemed well. He covered himself up and then even pulled the bedspread unusually high up over his shoulders. He looked up at George in a not unfriendly manner.

"You do still remember him, don't you?" said George, nodding his head in encouragement.

"Am I well covered up now?" asked the father, as if he could not check whether his feet were sufficiently tucked in.

"So you feel good in bed now," said George and arranged the bedding better around him.

"Am I well covered up?" the father asked once more and seemed particularly keen to hear the answer.

"Just rest for now. You're well covered up."

"No!" cried his father, cutting short George's answer to the question. He threw back the covers with such force that in an instant they had completely flown off, and he stood upright on the bed. He steadied himself with only one hand lightly touching the ceiling. "You wanted to cover me up—I know that, my little offspring—but I am not yet under the covers. And even if this is the last strength I have, it's enough for you, too much for you. Yes, I do know your friend. He'd be a son after my own heart. That's why you've been betraying him for years. Why else? Do you think I've not wept for him? That's the reason you lock yourself in your office—no one should disturb you, the boss is busy—that's the only way you can write your two-faced little letters to Russia. But fortunately no one has to teach a father to see through his son. Just now when you thought you'd brought him down, so far down that your buttocks could sit on him and he wouldn't move, at that point my son the gentleman has decided to get married!"

George looked up at the frightening spectre of his father. The friend in St. Petersburg, whom the father suddenly knew so well, seized his imagination as never before. He saw him lost in the broad expanse of Russia. He saw him at the door of an empty, plundered business. Among the wreckage of his shelves, the shattered goods, the collapsed gas brackets, he was still standing, but only just. Why did he have to go so far away!

"But look at me," cried his father, and George ran, almost distracted, to the bed to take everything in, but he faltered half way.

"Because she hoisted up her skirts," the father began in an affected tone, "because she hoisted up her skirts like this, the repulsive goose," and in order to imitate the action, he raised his shirt so high one could see the scar from his war years on his thigh, "because she hoisted her dress up like this and this, you chatted her up, and that's how you could satisfy yourself with her without being disturbed—you've disgraced our mother's memory, betrayed your friend, and stuck your father in bed, so he can't move. But he can move, can't he?"

And he stood completely unsupported and kicked his legs. He was radiant with insight.

George stood in a corner, as far away as possible from his father. A long time before he had firmly decided to observe everything closely, so he would not be surprised somehow by any devious attack, from behind or from above. Now he recalled again this long-forgotten decision and forgot it, like someone pulling a short thread through the eye of a needle.

"But now your friend hasn't been betrayed at all," cried the father —his forefinger, waving back and forth, emphasized the point. "I've been his on-the-spot representative here."

"You comedian!" George could not resist calling out. He recognized immediately how damaging that was and bit down on his tongue, only too late—his eyes froze—until he doubled up with pain.

"Yes, naturally I've been playing a comedy! Comedy! A fine word! What other consolation remained for an old widowed father? Tell me—and while you're answering still be my living son—what else was left to me in my back room, persecuted by a disloyal staff, old right down into to my bones? And my son goes merrily through the world, finishing off business deals which I had set up, falling over himself with delight, and walking away from your father with the tight-lipped face of an honourable gentleman! Do you think I didn't love you, me, the one from whom you came?"

"Now he'll bend forward," thought George. "What if he falls and breaks apart!" These words hissed through his head.

His father leaned forward but did not fall over. When George did not come closer, as he had expected, he straightened himself up again.

"Stay where you are. I don't need you! You think you still have the strength to come here and are holding yourself back only because that's what you want. But what if you're wrong! I am still much stronger than you. Perhaps all on my own I would have had to back off, but your mother gave me so much of her strength that I've established a splendid relationship with your friend and I have your customers here in my pocket!"

"He even has pockets in his shirt!" said George to himself and thought with this comment he could make his father look ridiculous to the whole world. He thought this for only a moment, because he constantly forgot everything.

"Just link arms with your fiancée and cross my path! I'll sweep her right from your side—you have no idea how!"

George made a grimace, as if he didn't believe that. The father merely nodded towards George's corner, emphasizing the truth of what he'd said.

"How you amused me today when you came and asked whether you should write to your friend about the engagement. For he knows everything, you stupid boy, he knows everything! I've been writing to him, because you forgot to take my writing things away from me. That's why he hasn't come for years. He knows everything a hundred times better than you do yourself. He crumples up your letters unread in his left hand, while in his right hand he holds my letters up to read."

In his enthusiasm he swung his arm over his head. "He knows everything a thousand times better," he shouted.

"Ten thousand times!" said George, in order to make his father appear foolish, but in his mouth the phrase had already acquired the deathliest of tones.

"For years now I've been watching out for you to come with this question! Do you think I'm concerned about anything else? Do you think I read the newspapers? There!" and he threw a newspaper page which had somehow been carried into the bed right at George—an old newspaper, the name of which was completely unknown to George.

"How long you've waited before reaching maturity! Your mother had to die. She could not experience the joyous day. Your friend is deteriorating in his Russia—three years ago he was already yellow enough to be thrown away, and, as for me, well, you see how things are with me. You've got eyes for that!"

"So you've been lying in wait for me," cried George.

In a pitying tone, his father said as an afterthought, "Presumably you wanted to say that earlier. But now it's totally irrelevant."

And in a louder voice: "So now you know what there was in the world outside of yourself. Up to this point you've known only about yourself! Essentially you've been an innocent child, but even more essentially you've been a devilish human being! And therefore understand this: I sentence you now to death by drowning!"

George felt himself hounded from the room. The crash with which his father fell onto the bed behind him he still carried in his ears as he left. On the staircase, where he raced down the steps as if it were an inclined plane, he surprised his cleaning woman, who was intending to tidy the apartment after the night before. "Jesus!" she cried and hid her face in her apron. But he was already past her. He leapt out the front door, driven across the roadway to the water. He was already clutching the railings the way a starving man grasps his food. He swung himself over, like the outstanding gymnast he had been in his youth, to his parents' pride. He was still holding on, his grip weakening, when between the railings he caught sight of a motor coach which would easily drown out the noise of his fall. He called out quietly, "Dear parents, I have always loved you nonetheless" and let himself drop.

At that moment an almost unending stream of traffic was going over the bridge.

THE HUNTER GRACCHUS[1]

Two boys were sitting on the wall by the jetty playing dice. A man was reading a newspaper on the steps of a monument in the shadow of a hero wielding a sabre. A young girl was filling her tub with water at a fountain. A fruit seller was lying close to his produce and looking out to sea. Through the empty openings of the door and window of a bar two men could be seen drinking wine in the back. The landlord was sitting at a table in the front dozing. A small boat glided lightly into the small harbour, as if it were being carried over the water. A man in a blue jacket climbed out onto land and pulled the ropes through the rings. Behind the man from the boat, two other men in dark coats with silver buttons carried a bier, on which, under a large silk scarf with a floral pattern and fringe, a person was obviously lying. No one bothered with the newcomers on the jetty, even when they set the bier down to wait for their helmsman, who was still working with the ropes. No one came up to them, no one asked them any questions, no one took a closer look at them.

The helmsman was further held up a little by a woman with dishevelled hair, who now appeared on deck with a child at her breast. Then he moved on, pointing to a yellowish, two-story house which rose close by, directly on the left near the water. The bearers took up their load and carried it through the low door furnished with slender columns. A small boy opened a window, noticed immediately how the group was disappearing into the house, and quickly shut the window again. The door now closed, as well. It had been fashioned with care out of black oak wood. A flock of doves, which up to this point had been flying around the bell tower, came down in front of the house. The doves gathered before the door, as if their food was stored inside the house. One flew right up to the first floor and pecked at the window pane. They were brightly coloured, well cared for, lively animals. With a large sweep of her hand the woman threw some seeds towards

[1]Written in 1917, but unpublished in Kafka's lifetime; first published in 1931 in the collection *Beim Bau der Chinesischen Mauer*.

them from the boat. They ate them up and then flew over to the woman.

A man in a top hat with a mourning ribbon came down one of the small, narrow, steeply descending lanes which led to the harbour. He looked around him attentively. Everything upset him. He winced at the sight of some garbage in a corner. There were fruit peels on the steps of the monument. As he went by, he pushed them off with his cane. He knocked on the door of the parlour, while at the same time taking off his top hat with his black-gloved right hand. It was opened immediately, and about fifty small boys, lined up in two rows in a long corridor, bowed to him.

The helmsman came down the stairs, welcomed the gentleman, and led him upstairs. On the first floor he accompanied him around the slight, delicately built balcony surrounding the court-yard, and, as the boys crowded behind them at a respectful dis-tance, both men stepped into a large cool room at the back of the house. From it one could not see a facing house, only a bare grey-black rock wall. Those who had carried the bier were busy setting up and lighting some long candles at its head. But these provided no light. They only made the previously still shadows positively jump and flicker across the walls. The shawl was pulled back off the bier. On it lay a man with wildly unkempt hair and beard and a brown skin—he looked rather like a hunter. He lay there mo-tionless, apparently without breathing, his eyes closed, although his surroundings were the only thing indicating that it could be a corpse.

The gentleman stepped over to the bier, laid a hand on the fore-head of the man lying there, then knelt down and prayed. The helmsman gave a sign to the bearers to leave the room. They went out, drove away the boys who had gathered outside, and shut the door. The gentleman, however, was apparently still not satisfied with this stillness. He looked at the helmsman. The latter under-stood and went through a side door into the next room. The man on the bier immediately opened his eyes, turned his face with a painful smile towards the gentleman, and said, "Who are you?"

Without any surprise, the gentleman got up from his kneeling position and answered, "The burgomaster of Riva." The man on the bier nodded, pointed to a chair by stretching his arm out feebly, and then, after the burgomaster had accepted his invitation, said, "Yes, I knew that, Burgomaster, but in the first moments I've always forgotten it all—everything is going in circles around me, and it's better for me to ask, even when I know everything. You also presumably know that I am the hunter Gracchus."

"Of course," said the burgomaster. "I received the news today, during the night. We had been sleeping for some time. Then around midnight my wife called, 'Salvatore'—that's my name—'look at the dove at the window!' It was really a dove, but as large as a rooster. It flew up to my ear and said, 'Tomorrow the dead hunter Gracchus is coming. Welcome him in the name of the city.'"

The hunter nodded and pushed the tip of his tongue between his lips. "Yes, the doves fly here before me. But do you believe, Burgomaster, that I am to remain in Riva?"

"That I cannot yet say," answered the burgomaster. "Are you dead?"

"Yes," said the hunter, "as you see. Many years ago—it must have been a great many years ago—I fell from a rock in the Black Forest—that's in Germany—as I was tracking a chamois. Since then I've been dead."

"But you are also alive," said the burgomaster.

"To a certain extent," said the hunter, "to a certain extent I am also alive. My death boat lost its way—a wrong turn of the helm, a moment when the helmsman was not paying attention, a diversion through my wonderful homeland—I don't know what it was. I only know that I remain on the earth and that since that time my boat has journeyed over earthly waters. So I—who only wanted to live in my own mountains—travel on after my death through all the countries of the earth."

"And have you no share in the world beyond?" asked the burgomaster wrinkling his brow.

The hunter answered, "I am always on the immense staircase leading up to it. I roam around on this infinitely wide flight of steps, sometimes up, sometimes down, sometimes to the right, sometimes to the left, always in motion. From being a hunter I've become a butterfly. Don't laugh."

"I'm not laughing," protested the burgomaster.

"That's very considerate of you," said the hunter. "I am always moving. But when I go through the greatest upward motion and the door is already shining right above me, I wake up on my old boat, still drearily stranded in some earthly stretch of water. The basic mistake of my earlier death smirks at me in my cabin. Julia, the wife of the helmsman, knocks and brings to me on the bier the morning drink of the country whose coast we are sailing by at the time. I lie on a wooden plank bed, wearing—I'm no delight to look at—a filthy shroud, my hair and beard, black and gray, are inextricably intertangled, my legs covered by a large silk women's scarf, with a floral pattern and long fringes. At my head stands a church candle which illuminates me. On the wall opposite me is a small picture, evidently of a bushman aiming his spear at me and concealing himself as much as possible behind a splendidly painted shield. On board ship one comes across many stupid pictures, but this is one of the stupidest. Beyond that my wooden cage is completely empty. Through a hole in the side wall the warm air of the southern nights comes in, and I hear the water lapping against the old boat.

"I have been lying here since the time when I—the still living hunter Gracchus—was pursuing a chamois to its home in the Black Forest and fell. Everything took place as it should. I followed, fell down, bled to death in a ravine, was dead, and this boat was supposed to carry me to the other side. I still remember how happily I stretched myself out here on the planking for the first time. The mountains have never heard me singing the way these four still shadowy walls did then.

"I had been happy to be alive and was happy to be dead. Before I came on board, I gladly threw away my rag-tag collection of guns and bags, and the hunting rifle which I had always carried proudly, and slipped into the shroud like a young girl into her wedding dress. Here I lay down and waited. Then the accident happened."

"A nasty fate," said the burgomaster, raising his hand in a gesture of deprecation, "and you are not to blame for it in any way?"

"No," said the hunter. "I was a hunter. Is there any blame in that? I was raised to be a hunter in the Black Forest, where at that time there were still wolves. I lay in wait, shot, hit the target, removed the skin—is there any blame in that? My work was blessed. 'The great hunter of the Black Forest'—that's what they called me. Is that something bad?"

"It not up to me to decide that," said the burgomaster, "but it seems to me as well that there's no blame there. But then who is to blame?"

"The boatswain," said the hunter. "No one will read what I write here, no one will come to help me. If people were assigned the task of helping me, all the doors of all the houses would remain closed, all the windows would be shut, they would all lie in bed, with sheets thrown over their heads, the entire earth would be a hostel for the night. And that makes good sense, for no one knows of me, and if he did, he would have no idea of where I was staying, and if he knew that, he would still not know how to keep me there, and so he would not know how to help me. The thought of wanting to help me is a sickness and has to be cured with bed rest.

"I know that, and so I do not cry out to summon help, even if at moments—as I have no self-control, for example, right now—I do think about that very seriously. But to get rid of such ideas I need only look around and recall where I am and where—and this I can assert with full confidence—I have lived for centuries."

"That's extraordinary," said the burgomaster, "extraordinary. And now are you intending to remain with us in Riva?"

"I have no intentions," said the hunter with a smile and, to make up for his mocking tone, laid a hand on the burgomaster's knee. "I am here. I don't know any more than that. There's nothing more I can do. My boat is without a helm—it journeys with the wind which blows in the deepest regions of death."

THE GREAT WALL OF CHINA[1]

The Great Wall of China was finished at its most northerly location. The construction work moved up from the south-east and south-west and joined at this point. This system of building in sections was also followed on a small scale within the two great armies of workers, the eastern and western armies. It was carried out in the following manner: groups of about twenty workers were formed, each of which had to take on a section of the wall, about five hundred metres long. A neighbouring group then built a wall of similar length to meet them. But then afterwards, when the sections were fully joined, construction was not continued on any further at the end of this thousand-metre section. Instead the groups of workers were shipped off again to build the wall in completely different regions. Naturally, with this method many large gaps arose, which were filled in only gradually and slowly, many of them not until after it had already been reported that the building of the wall was complete. In fact, there are said to be gaps which have never been built in at all, although that's merely an assertion which probably belongs among the many legends which have arisen about the structure and which, for individual people at least, are impossible to prove with their own eyes and according to their own standards, because the structure is so immense.

Now, at first one might think it would have been more advantageous in every way to build in continuous sections or at least continuously within two main sections. For the wall was conceived as a protection against the people of the north, as was commonly announced and universally known. But how can protection be provided by a wall which is not built continuously? In fact, not only can such a wall not protect, but the structure itself is in constant danger. Those parts of the wall left standing abandoned in deserted regions could always be destroyed easily by the nomads, especially by those back then who, worried about the

---

[1]Written in 1917, but not published in Kafka's lifetime; first published in 1931.

building of the wall, changed their place of residence with incredible speed, like grasshoppers, and thus perhaps had an even better overall view of how the construction was proceeding than we did, the people who built it. However, there was really no other way to carry out the construction except the way it happened. In order to understand this, one must consider the following: the wall was to become a protection for centuries; thus, the essential prerequisites for the work were the most careful construction, the use of the architectural wisdom of all known ages and peoples, and an enduring sense of personal responsibility in the builders. Of course, for the more humble tasks one could use ignorant day labourers from the people—the men, women, and children who offered their services for good money. But the supervision of even four day labourers required a knowledgeable man, an educated expert in construction, someone who was capable of feeling sympathy deep in his heart for what was at stake here. And the higher the challenge, the greater the demands. And such men were, in fact, available—if not the crowds of them which this construction could have used, at least in great numbers.

This work was not undertaken recklessly. Fifty years before the start of construction, it was announced throughout the whole region of China which was to be enclosed within the wall that architecture and especially masonry were the most important areas of knowledge, and everything else was recognized only to the extent that it had some relationship to those. I still remember very well how as small children who could hardly walk we stood in our teacher's little garden and had to construct a sort of wall out of pebbles, and how the teacher gathered up his coat and ran against the wall, naturally making everything collapse, and then scolded us so much for the weakness of our construction that we ran off in all directions howling to our parents. A tiny incident, but an indication of the spirit of the times.

I was lucky that at twenty years of age, when I passed the final examination of the lowest school, the construction of the wall was just starting. I say lucky because many who earlier had attained the highest limit of education available to them had no idea for years what to do with their knowledge and wandered around uselessly, with the most splendid architectural plans in their heads, and a great many of them just went downhill from there. But the ones who finally got to work as supervisors on the construction, even if they had the lowest rank, were really worthy of their position. They were masons who had given much thought to the construction and never stopped thinking about it, men who, right from the first stone which they let sink into the ground, had a sense of themselves as part of the wall. Such masons, of course, were driven not only by the desire to carry out the work as thoroughly as possible but also by impatience to see the structure finally standing there in its complete final perfection. Day labourers do not experience this impatience. They are driven only by their pay. The higher supervisors and, indeed, even the middle supervisors, see enough from their various perspectives of the growth of the wall to keep their spirits energized. But the subordinate supervisors, men who were mentally far above their outwardly trivial tasks, had to be catered to in other ways. One could not, for example, let them lay one building block on top of another in an uninhabited region of the mountains, hundreds of miles from their homes, for months or even years at a time. The hopelessness of such a hard task, which could not be completed even in a long human lifetime, would have caused them distress and, more than anything else, made them worthless for work. For that reason, the system of building in sections was chosen. Five hundred metres could be completed in something like five years, by which time naturally the supervisors were, as a rule, too exhausted and had lost all faith in themselves, in the building, and in the world. Thus, while they were still experiencing the elation of the celebrations for the joining up of a thousand metres of the wall, they were shipped far, far away. On their journey they saw here and there finished sections of the wall rising up; they passed through the quarters of the higher administrators, who gave them gifts as badges of honour, and they heard the rejoicing of new armies of workers streaming past them out of the depths of the land, saw forests being laid low, wood designated as scaffolding for the wall, witnessed mountains being broken up into rocks for the wall, and heard in the holy places the hymns of the pious praying for the construction to be finished. All this calmed their

34

impatience. The quiet life of home, where they spent some time, reinvigorated them. The high regard which all those doing the building enjoyed, the devout humility with which people listened to their reports, the trust which simple quiet citizens had that the wall would be completed someday—all this tuned the strings of their souls. Then, like eternally hopeful children, they took leave of their home. The enthusiasm for labouring once again at the people's work became irresistible. They set out from their houses earlier than necessary, and half the village accompanied them for a long way. On all the roads there were groups of people, pennants, banners—they had never seen how great and rich and beautiful and endearing their country was. Every countryman was a brother for whom they were building a protective wall and who would thank him with everything he had and was for all his life. Unity! Unity! Shoulder to shoulder, a coordinated movement of the people, their blood no longer confined in the limited circulation of the body but rolling sweetly and yet still returning through the infinite extent of China.

In view of all this, the system of piecemeal building becomes understandable. But there were still other reasons, too. And there is nothing strange in the fact that I have held off on this point for so long. It is the central issue in the whole construction of the wall, no matter how unimportant it appears at first. If I want to convey the ideas and experiences of that time and make them intelligible, I cannot probe deeply enough into this particular question.

First, it has to be said that achievements were brought to fruition at that time which rank slightly behind the Tower of Babel, although in the pleasure they gave to God, at least by human reckoning, they made an impression exactly the opposite of that structure. I mention this because at the time construction was beginning a scholar wrote a book in which he drew this comparison very precisely. In it he tried to show that the Tower of Babel had failed to attain its goal not at all for the reasons commonly asserted, or at least that the most important causes were not among these well-known ones. He not only based his proofs on texts and reports, but also claimed to have carried out personal inspections of the location and thus to have found that the structure collapsed and had to collapse because of the weakness of its foundation. And it is true that in this respect our age was far superior to that one long ago. Almost every educated person in our age was a mason by profession and infallible when it came to the business of laying foundations. But it was not at all the scholar's aim to prove this. Instead he claimed that the great wall alone would for the first time in the age of human beings create a secure foundation for a new Tower of Babel. So first the wall and then the tower. In those days the book was in everyone's hands, but I confess that even today I do not understand exactly how he imagined this tower. How could the wall, which never once took the form of a circle but only a sort of quarter or half circle, provide the foundation for a tower? But it could be meant only in a spiritual sense. But then why the wall, which was something real, a product of the efforts and lives of hundreds of thousands of people? And why were there plans in the book—admittedly hazy plans—sketching the tower, as well as detailed proposals about how the energies of the people could be strictly channelled into the new work in the future.

There was a great deal of mental confusion at the time—this book is only one example—perhaps for the simple reason that so many people were trying as hard as they could to join together for a single purpose. Human nature, which is fundamentally careless and by nature like the whirling dust, endures no restraint. If it restricts itself, it will soon begin to shake the restraints madly and tear up walls, chains, and even itself in every direction.

It is possible that even these considerations, which argued against building the wall in the first place, were not ignored by the leadership when they decided on piecemeal construction. We—and here I'm really speaking on behalf of many—actually first found out about it by spelling out the orders from the highest levels of management and learned for ourselves that without the leadership neither our school learning nor our human understanding would have been adequate for the small position we had within the enormous totality. In the office of the leadership—where it was and who sat there no one I asked knows or knew—in this office I imagine that all human thoughts and wishes revolve in a circle, and all human aims and fulfillments in a circle going in the opposite direction. But through the window the reflection of the divine worlds fell onto the hands of the leadership as they drew up the plans.

And for this reason the incorruptible observer will reject the notion that if the leadership had seriously wanted a continuous construction of the wall, they would not have been able to overcome the difficulties standing in the way. So the only conclusion left is that the leadership deliberately chose piecemeal construction. But building in sections was something merely makeshift and impractical. So the conclusion remains that the leadership wanted something impractical. An odd conclusion! True enough, and yet from another perspective it had some inherent justification. Nowadays one can perhaps speak about it without danger. At that time for many people, even the best, there was a secret principle: Try with all your powers to understand the orders of the leadership, but only up to a certain limit—then stop thinking about them. A very reasonable principle, which incidentally found an even wider interpretation in a later often repeated comparison: Stop further thinking, not because it could harm you—it is not at all certain that it will harm you. In this matter one cannot speak in general about harming or not harming. What will happen to you is like a river in spring. It rises, grows stronger, eats away more powerfully at the land along its banks, and still maintains its own course down to the sea and is more welcome as a fitter partner for the sea. Reflect upon the orders of the leadership as far as that. But then the river overflows its banks, loses its form and shape, slows down its forward movement, tries, contrary to its destiny, to form small seas inland, damages the fields, and yet cannot maintain its expansion long, but runs back within its banks, in fact, even dries up miserably in the hot time of year which follows. Do not reflect on the orders of the leadership to that extent.

Now, this comparison may perhaps have been extraordinarily apt during the construction of the wall, but it has at least only a limited relevance to my present report. For my investigation is merely historical. There is no lightning strike flashing any more from storm clouds which have long since vanished, and thus I may seek an explanation for the piecemeal construction which goes further than the one people were satisfied with back then. The limits which my ability to think sets for me are certainly narrow enough, but the region one would have to pass through here is endless.

Against whom was the great wall to provide protection? Against the people of the north. I come from south-east China. No northern people can threaten us there. We read about them in the books of the ancients. The atrocities which their nature prompts them to commit make us heave a sigh on our peaceful porches. In the faithfully accurate pictures of artists we see these faces of damnation, with their mouths flung open, the sharp pointed teeth stuck in their jaws, their straining eyes, which seem to be squinting for someone to seize, someone their jaws will crush and rip to pieces. When children are naughty, we hold up these pictures in front of them, and they immediately burst into tears and run into our arms. But we know nothing else about these northern lands. We have never seen them, and if we remain in our village, we never will see them, even if they charge straight at us and hunt us on their wild horses. The land is so huge, it would not permit them to reach us, and they would lose themselves in the empty air.

So if things are like this, why do we leave our homeland, the river and bridges, our mothers and fathers, our crying wives, our children in need of education, and go away to school in the distant city, with our thoughts on the wall to the north, even further away? Why? Ask the leadership. They know us. As they mull over their immense concerns, they know about us, understand our small worries, see us all sitting together in our humble huts, and approve or disapprove of the prayer which the father of the house says in the evening in the circle of his family. And if I may be permitted such ideas about the leadership, then I must say that in my view the leadership existed even earlier. It did not come together like some high mandarins quickly summoned to a meeting by a beautiful dream of the future, something hastily concluded, a meeting which by evening saw to it that the general population was driven from their beds by a knocking on the door, so that they could carry out the decision, even if it was only to set up a lantern in honour of a god who had shown favour to the masters the day before, so that he could thrash them in some dark corner the next day, when the lantern had only just died out. On the contrary, I imagine the leadership has existed since time immemorial, along with the decision to construct the wall as well. Innocent northern people believed they were the cause; the admirable and innocent emperor believed he had given orders for it. We who were builders of the wall know otherwise and are silent.

Even back then during the construction of the wall and afterwards, right up to the present day, I have devoted myself almost exclusively to the histories of different people. There are certain questions for which one can, to some extent, get to the heart of the matter only in this way. Using this method I have found that we Chinese possess certain popular and state institutions which are uniquely clear and, then again, others which are uniquely obscure. Tracking down the reasons for these, especially for the latter phenomena, always appealed to me, and still does, and the construction of the wall is fundamentally concerned with these issues.

Now, among our most obscure institutions one can certainly include the empire itself. Of course, in Peking, right in the court, there is some clarity about it, although even this is more apparent than real. And the teachers of constitutional law and history in the high schools give out that they are precisely informed about these things and that they are able to pass this knowledge on to their students. The deeper one descends into the lower schools, the more the doubts about the students' own knowledge understandably disappear, and a superficial education surges up as high as a mountain around a few precepts drilled into them for centuries, sayings which, in fact, have lost nothing of their eternal truth, but which remain also eternally unrecognized in this mist and fog.

But, in my view, it's precisely the empire we should be asking the people about, because in them the empire has its final support. It's true that in this matter I can speak once again only about my own homeland. Other than the agricultural deities and the service to them, which so beautifully and variously fills up the entire year, our thinking concerns itself only with the emperor. But not with the present emperor. We would have concerned ourselves with the present one if we had recognized who he was or had known anything definite about him. We were naturally always trying—and it's the single curiosity which consumed us—to find out something or other about him, but, no matter how strange this sounds, it was hardly possible to learn anything, either from pilgrims, even though they wandered through much of our land, or from the close or remote villages, or from boatmen, although they have travelled not merely on our little waterways but also on the sacred rivers. Of course, we heard a great deal, but could gather nothing from the many details.

Our land is so huge, that no fairy tale can adequately deal with its size. Heaven hardly covers it all. And Peking is only a point, the imperial palace only a tiny dot. It's true that, by contrast, throughout all the different levels of the world the emperor, as emperor, is great. But the living emperor, a human being like us, lies on a peaceful bed, just as we do. It is, no doubt, of ample proportions, but it could be merely narrow and short. Like us, he sometime stretches out his limbs and, if he is very tired, yawns with his delicately delineated mouth. But how are we to know about that thousands of miles to the south, where we almost border on the Tibetan highlands? Besides, any report which might come, even if it reached us, would get there much too late and would be long out of date. Around the emperor the glittering and yet murky court throngs—malice and enmity clothed as servants and friends, the counterbalance to the imperial power, with their poisoned arrows always trying to shoot the emperor down from his side of the balance scales. The empire is immortal, but the individual emperor falls and collapses. Even entire dynasties finally sink down and breathe their one last death rattle. The people will never know anything about these struggles and suffering.

Like those who have come too late, like strangers to the city, they stand at the end of the thickly populated side alleyways, quietly living off the provisions they have brought with them, while far off in the market place right in the middle foreground the execution of their master is taking place.

There is a legend which expresses this relationship well. The Emperor—so they say—has sent a message, directly from his death bed, to you alone, his pathetic subject, a tiny shadow which has taken refuge at the furthest distance from the imperial sun. He ordered the herald to kneel down beside his death bed and whispered the message to him. He thought it was so important that he had the herald repeat it back to him. He confirmed the accuracy of the verbal message by nodding his head. And in front of the entire crowd of those who have come to witness his death—all the obstructing walls have been broken down and all the great ones of his empire are standing in a circle on the broad and high soaring flights of stairs—in front of all of them he dispatched his herald. The messenger started off at once, a powerful, tireless man. Sticking one arm out and then another, he makes his way through the crowd. If he runs into resistance, he points to his breast where there is a sign of the sun. So he moves forward easily, unlike anyone else. But the crowd is so huge; its dwelling places are infinite. If there were an open field, how he would fly along, and soon you would hear the marvellous pounding of his fist on your door. But instead of that, how futile are all his efforts. He is still forcing his way through the private rooms of the innermost palace. He will never win his way through. And if he did manage that, nothing would have been achieved. He would have to fight his way down the steps, and, if he managed to do that, nothing would have been achieved. He would have to stride through the courtyards, and after the courtyards the second palace encircling the first, and, then again, stairs and courtyards, and then, once again, a palace, and so on for thousands of years. And if he finally did burst through the outermost door—but that can never, never happen—the royal capital city, the centre of the world, is still there in front of him, piled high and full of sediment. No one pushes his way through here, certainly not with a message from a dead man. But you sit at your window and dream to yourself of that message when evening comes.

That's exactly how our people look at the emperor, hopelessly and full of hope. They don't know which emperor is on the throne, and there are even doubts about the name of the dynasty. In the schools they learn a great deal about things like the succession, but the common uncertainty in this respect is so great that even the best pupils are drawn into it. In our villages emperors long since dead are set on the throne, and one of them who still lives on only in songs had one of his announcements issued a little while ago, which the priest read out from the altar. Battles from our most ancient history are now fought for the first time, and with a glowing face your neighbour charges into your house with the report. The imperial wives, overindulged on silk cushions, alienated from noble customs by shrewd courtiers, swollen with thirst for power, driven by greed, excessive in their lust, are always committing their evil acts over again. The further back they are in time, the more terrible all their colours glow, and with a loud cry of grief our village eventually gets to learn how an empress thousands of years ago drank her husband's blood in lengthy gulps.

That, then, is how the people deal with the rulers from the past, but they mix up the present rulers with the dead ones. If once, once in a person's lifetime an imperial official travelling around the province chances to come into our village, sets out some demands or other in the name of the rulers, checks the tax lists, attends a school class, interrogates the priest about our comings and goings, and then, before climbing into his sedan chair, summarizes everything in a long sermon to the assembled local population, at that point a smile crosses every face, one man looks furtively at another and bends over his children, so as not to let the official see him. How, people think, can he speak of a dead man as if he were alive. This emperor already died a long time ago, the dynasty has been extinguished, the official is having fun with us. But we'll act as if we didn't notice, so that we don't hurt his feelings. However, in all seriousness we'll obey only our present ruler, for anything else would be a sin. And behind the official's sedan chair as it hurries away there arises from the already decomposed urn someone high up who is arbitrarily endorsed as ruler of the village.

Similarly, with us people are, as a rule, little affected by political revolutions and contemporary wars. Here I recall an incident from my youth. In a neighbouring but still very far distant province a rebellion broke out. I cannot remember the causes any more. Besides, they are not important here. In that province reasons for rebellion arise every new day—they are an excitable people. Well, on one occasion a rebel pamphlet was brought into my father's house by a beggar who had travelled through that province. It happened to be a holiday. Our living room was full of guests. The priest sat in their midst and studied the pamphlet. Suddenly everyone started laughing, the sheet was torn to pieces in the general confusion, and the beggar, although he had already been richly rewarded, was chased out of the room with blows. Everyone scattered and ran out into the beautiful day. Why? The dialect of the neighbouring province is essentially different from ours, and these differences manifest themselves also in certain forms of the written language, which for us have an antiquated character. Well, the priest had scarcely read two pages like that, and people had already decided. Old matters heard long ago, and long since got over. And although—as I recall from my memory—a horrifying way of life seemed to speak irrefutably through the beggar, people laughed and shook their head and were unwilling to hear any more. That's how ready people are among us to obliterate the present.

If one wanted to conclude from such phenomena that we basically have no emperor at all, one would not be far from the truth. I need to say it again and again: There is perhaps no people more faithful to the emperor than we are in the south, but the emperor derives no benefits from our loyalty. It's true that on the way out of our village there stands on a little pillar the sacred dragon, which, for as long as men can remember, has paid tribute by blowing its fiery breath straight in the direction of Peking. But for the people in the village Peking itself is much stranger than living in the next world. Could there really be a village where houses stand right beside each other covering the fields and reaching further than the view from our hills, with men standing shoulder to shoulder between these houses day and night? Rather than imagining such a city, it's easier for us to believe that Peking and its emperor are one, something like a cloud, peacefully moving along under the sun as the ages pass.

Now, the consequence of such opinions is a life which is to some extent free and uncontrolled. Not in any way immoral—purity of morals like those in my homeland I have hardly ever come across in my travels. But nonetheless a way of life that stands under no present law and only pays attention to the wisdom and advice which reach across to us from ancient times.

I guard again generalizations and do not claim that things like this go on in all ten thousand villages of our province or, indeed, in all five hundred provinces of China. But on the basis of the many writings which I have read concerning this subject, as well as on the basis of my own observations, especially since with the construction of the wall the human material provided an opportunity for a man of feeling to travel through the souls of almost all the provinces—on the basis of all this perhaps I may state that with respect to the emperor the prevailing idea again and again reveals everywhere a certain essential feature common to the conception in my homeland. Now, I have no desire at all to let this conception stand as a virtue—quite the contrary. It's true that in the main things the blame rests with the government, which in the oldest empire on earth right up to the present day has not been able or has, among other things, neglected to cultivate the institution of empire sufficiently clearly so that it is immediately and ceaselessly effective right up to the most remote frontiers of the empire. On the other hand, however, there is in this also a weakness in the people's power of imagining or believing, which has not succeeded in pulling the empire out of its deep contemplative state in Peking and making it something fully vital and present in the hearts of subjects, who nonetheless want nothing better than to feel its touch once and then die from the experience.

So this conception is really not a virtue. It's all the more striking that this very weakness appears to be one of the most important ways of unifying our people. Indeed, if one may go so far as to use the expression, it is the very ground itself on which we live. To provide a detailed account of why we have a flaw here would amount not just to rattling our consciences but, what is much more serious, to making our legs tremble. And therefore I do not wish to go any further in the investigation of these questions at the present time.

A COUNTRY DOCTOR[1]

I was in great difficulty. An urgent journey was facing me. A seriously ill man was waiting for me in a village ten miles distant. A severe snowstorm filled the space between him and me. I had a carriage—a light one, with large wheels, entirely suitable for our country roads. Wrapped up in furs with the bag of instruments in my hand, I was already standing in the courtyard ready for the journey; but the horse was missing—the horse. My own horse had died the previous night, as a result of overexertion in this icy winter. My servant girl was at that very moment running around the village to see if she could borrow a horse, but it was hopeless—I knew that—and I stood there useless, increasingly covered with snow, becoming all the time more immobile. The girl appeared at the gate, alone. She was swinging the lantern. Of course, who is now going to lend his horse for such a journey? I walked once again across the courtyard. I couldn't see what to do. Distracted and tormented, I kicked my foot against the cracked door of the pig sty which had not been used for years. The door opened and banged to and fro on its hinges. A warmth and smell as if from horses came out. A dim stall lantern on a rope swayed inside. A man huddled down in the stall below showed his open blue-eyed face. "Shall I hitch up?" he asked, crawling out on all fours. I didn't know what to say and merely bent down to see what was still in the stall. The servant girl stood beside me. "One doesn't know the sorts of things one has stored in one's own house," she said, and we both laughed. "Hey, Brother, hey Sister," the groom cried out, and two horses, powerful animals with strong flanks, shoved their way one behind the other, legs close to the bodies, lowering their well-formed heads like camels, and getting through the door space, which they completely filled, only through the powerful movements of their rumps. But right away they stood up straight, long legged, with thick steaming bodies. "Help him," I said, and the girl obediently hurried to hand the wagon harness to the groom. But as soon as she was beside him, the groom puts his arms around her and pushes his face against hers. She screams out

[1]First published in *Die Neue Dichtung*, 1918

and runs over to me. On the girl's cheek are red marks from two rows of teeth. "You brute," I cry out in fury, "do you want the whip?" But I immediately remember that he is a stranger, that I don't know where he comes from, and that he's helping me out of his own free will, when everyone else is refusing to. As if he knows what I am thinking, he takes no offence at my threat, but turns around to me once more, still busy with the horses. Then he says, "Climb in," and, in fact, everything is ready. I notice that I have never before traveled with such a beautiful team of horses, and I climb in happily. "But I'll take the reins. You don't know the way," I say. "Of course," he says; "I'm not going with you. I'm staying with Rosa." "No," screams Rosa and runs into the house, with an accurate premonition of the inevitability of her fate. I hear the door chain rattling as she sets it in place. I hear the lock click. I see how in addition she chases down the corridor and through the rooms putting out all the lights in order to make herself impossible to find. "You're coming with me," I say to the groom, "or I'll give up the journey, no matter how urgent it is. It's not my intention to give you the girl as the price of the trip." "Giddy up," he says and claps his hands. The carriage is torn away, like a piece of wood in a current. I still hear how the door of my house is breaking down and splitting apart under the groom's onslaught, and then my eyes and ears are filled with a roaring sound which overwhelms all my senses at once. But only for a moment. Then I am already there, as if the farm yard of my invalid opens up immediately in front of my courtyard gate. The horses stand quietly. The snowfall has stopped, moonlight all around. The sick man's parents rush out of the house, his sister behind them. They almost lift me out of the carriage. I get nothing from their confused talking. In the sick room one can hardly breathe the air. The neglected cooking stove is smoking. I want to push open the window, but first I'll look at the sick man. Thin, without fever, not cold, not warm, with empty eyes, without a shirt, the young man under the stuffed quilt heaves himself up, hangs around my throat, and whispers in my ear, "Doctor, let me die." I look around. No one has heard. The parents stand silently, leaning forward, and wait for my judgment. The sister has brought a stool for

47

my handbag. I open the bag and look among my instruments. The young man constantly gropes at me from the bed to remind me of his request. I take some tweezers, test them in the candle light, and put them back. "Yes," I think blasphemously, "in such cases the gods do help. They send the missing horse, even add a second one because it's urgent, and even throw in a groom as a bonus." Now for the first time I think once more of Rosa. What am I doing? How am I saving her? How do I pull her out from under this groom, ten miles away from her, with uncontrollable horses in the front of my carriage? These horses, who have now somehow loosened their straps, are pushing open the window from outside, I don't know how. Each one is sticking its head through a window and, unmoved by the crying of the family, is observing the invalid. "I'll go back right away," I think, as if the horses were ordering me to journey back, but I allow the sister, who thinks I am in a daze because of the heat, to take off my fur coat. A glass of rum is prepared for me. The old man claps me on the shoulder; the sacrifice of his treasure justifies this familiarity. I shake my head. In the narrow circle of the old man's thinking I was not well; that's the only reason I refuse to drink. The mother stands by the bed and entices me over. I follow and, as a horse neighs loudly at the ceiling, lay my head on the young man's chest, which trembles under my wet beard. That confirms what I know: the young man is healthy. His circulation is a little off, saturated with coffee by his caring mother, but he's healthy and best pushed out of bed with a shove. I'm no improver of the world and let him lie there. I am employed by the district and do my duty to the full, right to the point where it's almost too much. Badly paid, but I'm generous and ready to help the poor. I still have to look after Rosa, and then the young man may have his way, and I want to die, too. What am I doing here in this endless winter! My horse is dead, and there is no one in the village who'll lend me his. I have to drag my team out of the pig sty. If they hadn't happened to be horses, I'd have had to travel with pigs. That's the way it is. And I nod to the family. They know nothing about it, and if they did know, they wouldn't believe it. Incidentally, it's easy to write prescriptions, but difficult to come to an understanding with people. Now, at this point my visit might have come to an end—they have once more called for my help unnecessarily. I'm used to that. With the help of my night bell the entire region torments me, but that this time I had to sacrifice Rosa as well, this beautiful girl, who lives in my house all year long and whom I scarcely notice—this sacrifice is too great, and I must somehow in my own head subtly rationalize it away for the moment, in order not to leave this family who cannot, even with their best will, give me Rosa back again. But as I am closing up my hand bag and calling for my fur coat, the family is standing together, the father sniffing the glass of rum in his hand, the mother, probably disappointed in me—what more do these people really expect?—tearfully biting her lips, and the sister flapping a very bloody hand towel, I am somehow ready, in the circumstances, to concede that the young man is perhaps nonetheless sick. I go to him. He smiles up at me, as if I was bringing him the most nourishing kind of soup—ah, now both horses are whinnying, the noise is probably supposed to come from higher regions in order to illuminate my examination—and now I find out that, yes indeed, the young man is ill. On his right side, in the region of the hip, a wound the size of the palm of one's hand has opened up. Rose coloured, in many different shadings, dark in the depths, brighter on the edges, delicately grained, with uneven patches of blood, open to the light like a mining pit. That's what it looks like from a distance. Close up a complication is apparent. Who can look at that without whistling softly? Worms, as thick and long as my little finger, themselves rose coloured and also spattered with blood, are wriggling their white bodies with many limbs from their stronghold in the inner of the wound towards the light. Poor young man, there's no helping you. I have found out your great wound. You are dying from this flower on your side. The family is happy; they see me doing something. The sister says that to the mother, the mother tells the father, the father tells a few guests who are coming in on tiptoe through the moonlight of the open door, balancing themselves with outstretched arms. "Will you save me?" whispers the young man, sobbing, quite blinded by the life inside his wound. That's how people are in my region. Always demanding the impossible from the doctor. They have lost the old faith. The priest sits at home and tears his religious robes to pieces, one after the other. But the doctor is supposed to achieve everything with his delicate surgeon's hand. Well, it's what they like to think. I have not offered myself. If they use me for sacred purposes, I let that happen to me as well. What more do I want, an old country doctor, robbed of my servant girl! And they come, the family and the village elders, and are taking my clothes off. A choir of school children with the teacher at the head stands in front of the house and sings an extremely simple melody with the words

> Take his clothes off, then he'll heal,
> and if he doesn't cure, then kill him.
> It's only a doctor; it's only a doctor.

Then I am stripped of my clothes and, with my fingers in my beard and my head tilted to one side, I look at the people quietly. I am completely calm and clear about everything and stay that way, too, although it is not helping me at all, for they are now taking me by the head and feet and dragging me into the bed. They lay me against the wall on the side of wound. Then they all go out of the room. The door is shut. The singing stops. Clouds move in front of the moon. The bedclothes lie warmly around me. In the open space of the windows the horses' heads sway like shadows. "Do you know," I hear someone saying in my ear, "my confidence in you is very small. You were only shaken out from somewhere. You don't come on your own feet. Instead of helping, you give me less room on my deathbed. The best thing would be if I scratch your eyes out." "Right," I say, "it's a disgrace. But now I'm a doctor. What am I supposed to do? Believe me, things are not easy for me either." "Should I be satisfied with this excuse? Alas, I'll probably have to be. I always have to make do. I came into the world with a beautiful wound; that was all I was furnished with." "Young friend," I say, "your mistake is that you have no perspective. I've already been in all the sick rooms, far and wide, and I tell you your wound is not so bad. Made in a tight corner with two blows from an axe. Many people offer their side and hardly hear the axe in the forest, to say nothing of the fact that it's coming closer to them." "Is that really so, or are you deceiving me in my fever?" "It is truly so. Take the word of honour of a medical doctor." He took my word and grew still. But now it was time to think about my escape. The horses were still standing loyally in their place. Clothes, fur coat, and bag were quickly gathered up. I didn't want to delay by getting dressed; if the horses rushed as they had on the journey out, I should, in fact, be springing out of that bed into my own, as it were. One horse obediently pulled back from the window. I threw the bundle into the carriage. The fur coat flew too far and was caught on a hook by only one arm. Good enough. I swung myself up onto the horse. The reins dragging loosely, one horse barely harnessed to the other, the carriage swaying behind, last of all the fur coat in the snow. "Giddy up," I said, but there was no giddying up about it. We dragged slowly through the snowy desert like old men; for a long time the fresh but inaccurate singing of the children resounded behind us:

> "Enjoy yourselves, you patients.
> The doctor's laid in bed with you."

I'll never come home at this rate. My flourishing practice is lost. A successor is robbing me, but to no avail, for he cannot replace me. In my house the disgusting groom is wreaking havoc. Rosa is his victim. I will not think it through. Naked, abandoned to the frost of this unhappy age, with an earthly carriage and unearthly horses, I drive around by myself, an old man. My fur coat hangs behind the wagon, but I cannot reach it, and no one from the nimble rabble of patients lifts a finger. Betrayed! Betrayed! Once one responds to a false alarm on the night bell, there's no making it good again—not ever.

A REPORT FOR AN ACADEMY[1]

Esteemed Gentlemen of the Academy!

You show me the honour of calling upon me to submit a report to the Academy concerning my previous life as an ape.

In this sense, unfortunately, I cannot comply with your request. Almost five years separate me from my existence as an ape, a short time perhaps when measured by the calendar, but endlessly long to gallop through, as I have done, at times accompanied by splendid people, advice, applause, and orchestral music, but basically alone, since all those accompanying me held themselves back a long way from the barrier, in order to preserve the image. This achievement would have been impossible if I had stubbornly wished to hold onto my origin, onto the memories of my youth. Giving up that obstinacy was, in fact, the highest command that I gave myself. I, a free ape, submitted myself to this yoke. In so doing, however, my memories for their part constantly closed themselves off against me. If people had wanted it, my journey back at first would have been possible through the entire gateway which heaven builds over the earth, but as my development was whipped onwards, the gate simultaneously grew lower and narrower all the time. I felt myself more comfortable and more enclosed in the world of human beings. The storm which blew me out of my past eased off. Today it is only a gentle breeze which cools my heels. And the distant hole through which it comes and through which I once came has become so small that, even if I had sufficient power and will to run back there, I would have to scrape the fur off my body in order to get through. Speaking frankly, as much as I like choosing metaphors for these things— speaking frankly: your experience as apes, gentlemen—to the extent that you have something of that sort behind you—cannot be more distant from you than mine is from me. But it tickles at

[1]First published in *Der Jude*, November 1917. In addition to the main dramatic narrative, Kafka manuscripts include two short fragments on the "Red Peter" theme. These have not been included here.

the heels of everyone who walks here on earth, the small chimpanzee as well as the great Achilles.

In the narrowest sense, however, I can perhaps answer your question, nonetheless, and indeed I do so with great pleasure.

The first thing I learned was to give a handshake. The handshake
displays candour. Today, when I stand at the pinnacle of my
career, may I add to that first handshake also my candid words.
For the Academy it will not provide anything essentially new and
will fall far short of what people have asked of me and what with
the best will I cannot speak about—but nonetheless it should
demonstrate the direct line by which someone who was an ape
was forced into the world of men and which he has continued
there. Yet I would certainly not permit myself to say even the
trivial things which follow if I were not completely sure of myself
and if my position on all the great music hall stages of the civi-
lized world had not established itself unassailably.

I come from the Gold Coast. For an account of how I was captured
I rely on the reports of strangers. A hunting expedition from the
firm of Hagenbeck—incidentally, since then I have already emptied a number of bottles of good red wine with the leader of that
expedition—lay hidden in the bushes by the shore when I ran
down in the evening in the middle of a band of apes for a drink.
Someone fired a shot. I was the only one struck. I received two
hits.

One was in the cheek—that was superficial. But it left behind a
large hairless red scar which earned me the name Red Peter—a
revolting name, completely inappropriate, presumably something
invented by an ape, as if the only difference between me and the
recently deceased trained ape Peter, who was well known here
and there, was the red patch on my cheek. But this is only by the
way.

The second shot hit me below the hip. It was serious. It's the reason that today I still limp a little. Recently I read in an article by
one of the ten thousand gossipers who vent their opinions about

me in the newspapers that my ape nature is not yet entirely repressed. The proof is that when visitors come I take pleasure in pulling off my trousers to show the entry wound caused by this shot. That fellow should have each finger of his writing hand shot off one by one. So far as I am concerned, I may pull my trousers down in front of anyone I like. People will not find there anything other than well cared for fur and the scar from—let us select here a precise word for a precise purpose, something that will not be misunderstood—the scar from a wicked shot. Everything is perfectly open; there is nothing to hide. When it comes to a question of the truth, every great mind discards the most subtle refinements of manners. However, if that writer were to pull down his trousers when he gets a visitor, that would certainly produce a different sight, and I'll take it as a sign of reason that he does not do that. But then he should not bother me with his delicate sensibilities.

After those shots I woke up—and here my own memory gradually begins—in a cage between decks on the Hagenbeck steamship. It was no four-sided cage with bars, but only three walls fixed to a crate, so that the crate constituted the fourth wall. The whole thing was too low to stand upright and too narrow for sitting down. So I crouched with bent knees, which shook all the time, and since at first I probably did not wish to see anyone and to remain constantly in the darkness, I turned towards the crate, while the bars of the cage cut into the flesh on my back. People consider such confinement of wild animals beneficial in the very first period of time, and today I cannot deny, on the basis of my own experience, that in a human sense that is, in fact, the case.

But at that time I didn't think about that. For the first time in my life I was without a way out—at least there was no direct way out. Right in front of me was the crate, its boards fitted closely together. Well, there was a hole running right through the boards. When I first discovered it, I welcomed it with a blissfully happy howl of ignorance. But this hole was not nearly big enough to stick my tail through, and all the power of an ape could not make it any bigger.

According to what I was told later, I am supposed to have made remarkably little noise. From that people concluded that either I must soon die or, if I succeeded in surviving the first critical period, I would be very capable of being trained. I survived this period. Muffled sobbing, painfully searching out fleas, wearily licking a coconut, banging my skull against the wall of the crate, sticking out my tongue when anyone came near me—these were the first occupations in my new life. In all of them, however, there was only one feeling: no way out. Nowadays, of course, I can portray those ape-like feelings only with human words and, as a result, I misrepresent them. But even if I can no longer attain the old truth of the ape, at least it lies in the direction I have described—of that there is no doubt.

Up until then I had had so many ways out, and now I no longer had one. I was tied down. If they had nailed me down, my freedom to move would not have been any less. And why? If you scratch raw the flesh between your toes, you won't find the reason. If you press your back against the bars of the cage until it almost slices you in two, you won't find the answer. I had no way out, but I had to come up with one for myself. For without that I could not live. Always in front of that crate wall—I would inevitably have died a miserable death. But according to Hagenbeck, apes belong at the crate wall—well, that meant I would cease being an ape. A clear and beautiful train of thought, which I must have planned somehow with my belly, since apes think with their bellies.

I'm worried that people do not understand precisely what I mean by a way out. I use the word in its most common and fullest sense. I am deliberately not saying freedom. I do not mean this great feeling of freedom on all sides. As an ape, I perhaps recognized it, and I have met human beings who yearn for it. But as far as I am concerned, I did not demand freedom either then or today. Incidentally, among human beings people all too often are deceived by freedom. And since freedom is reckoned among the most sublime feelings, the corresponding disappointment is also among the most sublime. In the variety shows, before my entrance, I have often watched a pair of artists busy on trapezes high up in the roof. They swung themselves, they rocked back and forth, they jumped, they hung in each other's arms, one held the other by clenching the hair with his teeth. "That, too, is human freedom," I thought, "self-controlled movement." What a mockery of sacred nature! At such a sight, no structure would stand up to the laughter of the apes.

No, I didn't want freedom. Only a way out—to the right or left or anywhere at all. I made no other demands, even if the way out should also be only an illusion. The demand was small; the disappointment would not be any greater—to move on further, to move on further! Only not to stand still with arms raised, pressed again a crate wall.

Today I see clearly that without the greatest inner calm I would never have been able to get out. And, in fact, I probably owe everything that I have become to the calmness which came over me after the first days there on the ship. And, in turn, I owe that calmness to the people on the ship.

They are good people, in spite of everything. Today I still enjoy remembering the clang of their heavy steps, which used to echo then in my half sleep. They had the habit of tackling everything extremely slowly. If one of them wanted to rub his eyes, he raised his hand as if it were a hanging weight. Their jokes were gross but hearty. Their laughter was always mixed with a rasp which sounded dangerous but meant nothing. They always had something in their mouths to spit out, and they didn't care where they spat. They always complained that my fleas sprung over onto them, but they were never seriously angry at me because of it. They even knew that fleas liked being in my fur and that fleas are jumpers. They learned to live with that. When they had no duties, sometimes a few of them sat down in a semi-circle around me. They didn't speak much, but only made noises to each other and smoked their pipes, stretched out on the crates. They slapped their knees as soon as I made the slightest movement, and from time to time one of them would pick up a stick and tickle me where I liked it. If I were invited today to make a journey on that ship, I would certainly decline the invitation, but it's equally certain that the memories I could dwell on of the time there between the decks would not be totally hateful.

The calmness which I acquired in this circle of people prevented me above all from any attempt to escape. Looking at it nowadays, it seems to me as if I had at least sensed that I had to find a way out if I wanted to live, but that this way out could not be reached by escaping. I no longer know if escape was possible, but I think it was: for an ape it should always be possible to flee. With my present teeth I have to be careful even with the ordinary task of cracking a nut, but then I must have been able, over time, to succeed in chewing through the lock on the door. I didn't do that. What would I have achieved by doing it? No sooner would I have stuck my head out, than they would have captured me again and locked me up in an even worse cage. Or I could have taken refuge unnoticed among the other animals—say, the boa constrictors opposite me—and breathed my last in their embraces. Or I could have managed to steal way up to the deck and to jump overboard. Then I'd have tossed back and forth for a little while on the ocean and would have drowned. Acts of despair. I did not think things through in such a human way, but under the influence of my surroundings conducted myself as if I had worked things out.

I did not work things out, but I did observe things with complete tranquility. I saw these men going back and forth, always the same faces, the same movements. Often it seemed to me as if there was only one man. So the man or these men went undisturbed. A lofty purpose dawned on me. No one promised me that if I could become like them the cage would be removed. Such promises, apparently impossible to fulfill, are not made. But if one makes the fulfillment good, then later the promises appear precisely there where one had looked for them earlier without success. Now, these men in themselves were nothing which attracted me very much. If I had been a follower of that freedom I just mentioned, I would certainly have preferred the ocean to the way out displayed in the dull gaze of these men. But in any case, I observed them for a long time before I even thought about such things—in fact, the accumulated observations first pushed me in the proper direction.

It was so easy to imitate these people. I could already spit on the first day. Then we used to spit in each other's faces. The only difference was that I licked my face clean afterwards. They did not. Soon I was smoking a pipe like an old man, and if I then also pressed my thumb down into the bowl of the pipe, the entire area between decks cheered. Still, for a long time I did not understand the difference between an empty and a full pipe.

I had the greatest difficulty with the bottle of alcohol. The smell was torture to me. I forced myself with all my power, but weeks went by before I could overcome my reaction. Curiously enough, the people took this inner struggle more seriously than anything else about me. In my memories I don't distinguish the people, but there was one who always came back, alone or with comrades, day and night, at very different times. He'd stand with the bottle in front of me and give me instructions. He did not understand me. He wanted to solve the riddle of my being. He used to uncork the bottle slowly and then look at me, in order to test if I had understood. I confess that I always looked at him with wildly overeager attentiveness. No human teacher has ever found on the entire earthly globe such a student of human beings. After he'd uncorked the bottle, he'd raise it to his mouth. I'd gaze at him, right into his throat. He would nod, pleased with me, and set the bottle to his lips. Delighted with my gradual understanding, I'd squeal and scratch myself all over, wherever it was convenient. He was happy. He'd set the bottle to his mouth and take a swallow. Impatient and desperate to emulate him, I would defecate over myself in my cage—and that again gave him great satisfaction. Then, holding the bottle at arm's length and bringing it up once more with a swing, he'd drink it down with one gulp, exaggerating his backward bending as a way of instructing me. Exhausted with so much great effort, I could no longer follow and would hang weakly onto the bars, while he ended the theoretical lesson by rubbing his belly and grinning.

Now the practical exercises first began. Was I not already too tired out by the theoretical part? Yes, indeed, far too weary. That's part of my fate. Nonetheless, I'd grab the proffered bottle as well as I could and uncork it trembling. Once I'd managed to do that, new energies would gradually take over. I lifted the bottle—with hardly any difference between me and the original—put it to my lips—and throw it away in disgust, in disgust, although it was empty and filled only with the smell, throw it with disgust onto the floor. To the sorrow of my teacher, to my own greater sorrow. And I still did not console him or myself when, after throwing away the bottle, I did not forget to give my belly a splendid rub and to grin as I did so.

All too often, the lesson went that way. And to my teacher's credit, he was not angry with me. Well, sometimes he held his burning pipe against my fur in some place or other which I could reach only with difficulty, until it began to burn. But then he would put it out himself with his huge good hand. He wasn't angry with me. He realized that we were fighting on the same side against ape nature and that I had the more difficult part.

It was certainly a victory for him and for me when one evening in front of a large circle of onlookers—perhaps it was a celebration, a gramophone was playing, an officer was wandering around among the people—when on this evening, at a moment when no one was watching, I grabbed a bottle of alcohol which had been inadvertently left standing in front of my cage, uncorked it just as I had been taught, amid the rising attention of the group, set it against my mouth and, without hesitating, with my mouth making no grimace, like an expert drinker, with my eyes rolling around, splashing the liquid in my throat, I really and truly drank the bottle empty, and then threw it away, no longer in despair, but like an artist. Well, I did forget to scratch my belly. But instead of that, because I couldn't do anything else, because I had to, because my senses were roaring, I cried out a short and good "Hello!" breaking out into human sounds. And with this cry I sprang into the community of human beings, and I felt its echo—"Just listen. He's talking!"—like a kiss on my entire sweat-soaked body.

I'll say it again: imitating human beings was not something which pleased me. I imitated them because I was looking for a way out, for no other reason. And even in that victory little was achieved. My voice immediately failed me again. It first came back months later. My distaste for the bottle of alcohol became even stronger. But at least my direction was given to me once and for all.

When I was handed over in Hamburg to my first trainer, I soon realized the two possibilities open to me: the zoological garden or the music hall. I did not hesitate. I said to myself: use all your energy to get into the Music Hall. That is the way out. The zoological garden is only a new barred cage. If you go there, you're lost.

And I learned, gentlemen. Alas, one learns when one has to. One learns when one wants a way out. One learns ruthlessly. One supervises oneself with a whip and tears oneself apart at the slightest resistance. My ape nature ran off, head over heels, out of me, so that in the process my first teacher himself almost became an ape and soon had to give up training and be carried off to a mental hospital. Fortunately he was soon discharged again.

But I went through many teachers—indeed, even several teachers at once. As I became even more confident of my abilities and the general public followed my progress and my future began to brighten, I took on teachers myself, let them sit down in five interconnected rooms, and studied with them all simultaneously, by constantly leaping from one room into another.

And such progress! The penetrating effects of the rays of knowledge from all sides on my awaking brain! I don't deny the fact—I was delighted with it. But I also confess that I did not overestimate it, not even then, even less today. With an effort which up to this point has never been repeated on earth, I have attained the average education of a European man. That would perhaps not amount to much, but it is something insofar as it helped me out of the cage and created this special way out for me—the way out of human beings. There is an excellent German expression: to beat one's way through the bushes. That I have done. I have beaten my way through the bushes. I had no other way, always assuming that freedom was not a choice.

If I review my development and its goal up to this point, I do not complain, but I not am content. With my hands in my trouser pockets, the bottle of wine on the table, I half lie and half sit in my rocking chair and gaze out the window. If I have a visitor, I welcome him as is appropriate. My impresario sits in the parlour. If I ring, he comes and listens to what I have to say. In the evening I almost always have a performance, and my success could hardly rise any higher. When I come home late at night from banquets, from scientific societies, or from social gatherings in someone's home, a small half-trained female chimpanzee is waiting for me, and I take my pleasure with her the way apes do. During the day I don't want to see her. For she has in her gaze the madness of a bewildered trained animal. I'm the only one who recognizes that, and I cannot bear it.

On the whole, at any rate, I have achieved what I wished to achieve. You shouldn't say it was not worth the effort. In any case, I don't want any human being's judgment. I only want to expand knowledge. I simply report. Even to you, esteemed gentlemen of the Academy, I have only made a report.

A HUNGER ARTIST[1]

In the last decades interest in hunger artists has declined considerably. Whereas in earlier days there was good money to be earned putting on major productions of this sort under one's own management, nowadays that is totally impossible. Those were different times. Back then the hunger artist captured the attention of the entire city. From day to day while the fasting lasted, participation increased. Everyone wanted to see the hunger artist at least once a day. During the later days there were people with subscription tickets who sat all day in front of the small barred cage. And there were even viewing hours at night, their impact heightened by torchlight. On fine days the cage was dragged out into the open air, and then the hunger artist was put on display particularly for the children. While for grown-ups the hunger artist was often merely a joke, something they participated in because it was fashionable, the children looked on amazed, their mouths open, holding each other's hands for safety, as he sat there on scattered straw—spurning a chair—in black tights, looking pale, with his ribs sticking out prominently, sometimes nodding politely, answering questions with a forced smile, even sticking his arm out through the bars to let people feel how emaciated he was, but then completely sinking back into himself, so that he paid no attention to anything, not even to what was so important to him, the striking of the clock, which was the single furnishing in the cage, but merely looking out in front of him with his eyes almost shut and now and then sipping from a tiny glass of water to moisten his lips.

Apart from the changing groups of spectators there were also constant observers chosen by the public—strangely enough they were usually butchers—who, always three at a time, were given the task of observing the hunger artist day and night, so that he didn't get anything to eat in some secret manner. It was, however, merely a formality, introduced to reassure the masses, for those who understood knew well enough that during the period of fasting the hunger artist would never, under any circumstances,

[1]First published in *Die neue Rundschau*, October 1922.

have eaten the slightest thing, not even if compelled by force. The honour of his art forbade it. Naturally, none of the watchers understood that. Sometimes there were nightly groups of watchers who carried out their vigil very laxly, deliberately sitting together in a distant corner and putting all their attention into playing cards there, clearly intending to allow the hunger artist a small refreshment, which, according to their way of thinking, he could get from some secret supplies. Nothing was more excruciating to the hunger artist than such watchers. They depressed him. They made his fasting terribly difficult. Sometimes he overcame his weakness and sang during the time they were observing, for as long as he could keep it up, to show people how unjust their suspicions about him were. But that was little help. For then they just wondered among themselves about his skill at being able to eat even while singing. He much preferred the observers who sat down right against the bars and, not satisfied with the dim back-lighting of the room, illuminated him with electric flashlights, which the impresario made available to them. The glaring light didn't bother him in the slightest. Generally he couldn't sleep at all, and he could always doze off a little under any lighting and at any hour, even in an overcrowded, noisy auditorium. With such observers, he was very happily prepared to spend the entire night without sleeping. He was ready to joke with them, to recount stories from his nomadic life and then, in turn, to listen to their stories—doing everything just to keep them awake, so that he could keep showing them once again that he had nothing to eat in his cage and that he was fasting as none of them could. He was happiest, however, when morning came and a lavish breakfast was brought for them at his own expense, on which they hurled themselves with the appetite of healthy men after a hard night's work without sleep. True, there were still people who wanted to see in this breakfast an unfair means of influencing the observers, but that was going too far, and if they were asked whether they wanted to undertake the observers' night shift for its own sake, without the breakfast, they excused themselves. But nonetheless they stood by their suspicions.

However, it was, in general, part of fasting that these doubts were inextricably associated with it. For, in fact, no one was in a position to spend time watching the hunger artist every day and night without interruption, so no one could know, on the basis of his own observation, whether this was a case of truly continuous, flawless fasting. The hunger artist himself was the only one who could know that and, at the same time, the only spectator capable of being completely satisfied with his own fasting. But the reason he was never satisfied was something different. Perhaps it was not fasting at all which made him so very emaciated that many people, to their own regret, had to stay away from his performance, because they couldn't bear to look at him. For he was also so skeletal out of dissatisfaction with himself, because he alone knew something that even initiates didn't know—how easy it was to fast. It was the easiest thing in the world. About this he did not remain silent, but people did not believe him. At best they thought he was being modest. Most of them, however, believed he was a publicity seeker or a total swindler, for whom, at all events, fasting was easy, because he understood how to make it easy, and then still had the nerve to half admit it. He had to accept all that. Over the years he had become accustomed to it. But this dissatisfaction kept gnawing at his insides all the time and never yet—and this one had to say to his credit—had he left the cage of his own free will after any period of fasting. The impresario had set the maximum length of time for the fast at forty days—he would never allow the fasting go on beyond that point, not even in the cosmopolitan cities. And, in fact, he had a good reason. Experience had shown that for about forty days one could increasingly whip up a city's interest by gradually increasing advertising, but that then the public turned away—one could demonstrate a significant decline in popularity. In this respect, there were, of course, small differences among different towns and among different countries, but as a rule it was true that forty days was the maximum length of time. So then on the fortieth day the door of the cage—which was covered with flowers—was opened, an enthusiastic audience filled the amphitheatre, a military band played, two doctors entered the cage, in order to take the necessary measurements of the hunger artist, the results were announced to the auditorium through a megaphone, and finally two young ladies arrived, happy about the fact that they were the ones who had just been selected by lot, and sought to lead the hunger artist down a couple of steps out of the cage, where on a small table a carefully chosen hospital meal was laid out. And at this moment the hunger artist always fought back. Of course, he still freely laid his bony arms in the helpful outstretched hands of the ladies bending over him, but he did not want to stand up. Why stop right now after forty days? He could have kept going for even longer, for an unlimited length of time. Why stop right now, when he was in his best form, indeed, not yet even in his best fasting form? Why did people want to rob him of the fame of fasting longer, not just so that he could become the greatest hunger artist of all time, which, in fact, he probably was already, but also so that he could surpass himself in some unimaginable way, for he felt there were no limits to his capacity for fasting? Why did this crowd, which pretended to admire him so much, have so little patience with him? If he kept going and kept fasting even longer, why would they not tolerate it? Then, too, he was tired and felt good sitting in the straw. Now he was supposed to stand up straight and tall and go to eat, something which, when he merely imagined it, made him feel nauseous right away. With great difficulty he repressed mentioning this only out of consideration for the women. And he looked up into the eyes of these women, apparently so friendly but in reality so cruel, and shook his excessively heavy head on his feeble neck. But then happened what always happened. The impresario came forward without a word—the music made talking impossible—raised his arms over the hunger artist, as if inviting heaven to look upon its work here on the straw, this unfortunate martyr, something the hunger artist certainly was, only in a completely different sense, grabbed the hunger artist around his thin waist, in the process wanting with his exaggerated caution to make people believe that here he had to deal with something fragile, and handed him over—not without secretly shaking him a little, so that the hunger artist's legs and upper body swung back and forth uncontrollably—to the wo-

A HUNGER ARTIST

men, who had in the meantime turned as pale as death. At this point, the hunger artist endured everything. His head lay on his chest—it was as if it had inexplicably rolled around and just stopped there—his body was arched back, his legs, in an impulse of self-preservation, pressed themselves together at the knees, but scraped the ground, as if they were not really on the floor but were looking for the real ground, and the entire weight of his body, admittedly very small, lay against one of the women, who appealed for help with flustered breath, for she had not imagined her post of honour would be like this, and then stretched her neck as far as possible, to keep her face from the least contact with the hunger artist, but then, when she couldn't manage this and her more fortunate companion didn't come to her assistance but trembled and remained content to hold in front of her the hunger artist's hand, that small bundle of knuckles, she broke into tears, to the delighted laughter of the auditorium, and had to be relieved by an attendant who had been standing ready for some time. Then came the meal. The impresario put a little food into the mouth of the hunger artist, now dozing as if he were fainting, and kept up a cheerful patter designed to divert attention away from the hunger artist's condition. Then a toast was proposed to the public, which was supposedly whispered to the impresario by the hunger artist, the orchestra confirmed everything with a great fanfare, people dispersed, and no one had the right to be dissatisfied with the event, no one except the hunger artist—he was always the only one.

He lived this way, taking small regular breaks, for many years, apparently in the spotlight, honoured by the world, but for all that, his mood was usually gloomy, and it kept growing gloomier all the time, because no one understood how to take it seriously. But how was he to find consolation? What was there left for him to wish for? And if a good-natured man who felt sorry for him ever wanted to explain to him that his sadness probably came from his fasting, then it could happen, especially at an advanced stage of the fasting, that the hunger artist responded with an outburst of rage and began to shake the cage like an animal, frightening everyone. But the impresario had a way of punishing moments like this, something he was happy to use. He would make an apology for the hunger artist to the assembled public, conceding that the irritability had been provoked only by his fasting, which well-fed people did not readily understand and which was capable of excusing the behaviour of the hunger artist. From there he would move on to speak about the equally hard to understand claim of the hunger artist that he could go on fasting for much longer than he was doing. He would praise the lofty striving, the good will, and the great self-denial no doubt contained in this claim, but then would try to contradict it simply by producing photographs, which were also on sale, for in the pictures one could see the hunger artist on the fortieth day of his fast, in bed, almost dead from exhaustion. Although the hunger artist was very familiar with this perversion of the truth, it always strained his nerves again and was too much for him. What was a result of the premature ending of the fast people were now proposing as its cause! It was impossible to fight against this lack of understanding, against this world of misunderstanding. In good faith he always still listened eagerly to the impresario at the bars of his cage, but each time, once the photographs came out, he would let go of the bars and, with a sigh, sink back into the straw, and a reassured public could come up again and view him.

When those who had witnessed such scenes thought back on them a few years later, often they were unable to understand themselves. For in the meantime that change mentioned above had set it. It happened almost immediately. There may have been more profound reasons for it, but who bothered to discover what they were? At any rate, one day the pampered hunger artist saw himself abandoned by the crowd of pleasure seekers, who preferred to stream to other attractions. The impresario chased around half of Europe one more time with him, to see whether he could still re-discover the old interest here and there. It was all futile. It was as if a secret agreement against the fasting performances had really developed everywhere. Naturally, the truth is that it could not have happened so quickly, and people later remembered some things which in the days of intoxicating success they had not paid sufficient attention to, some inadequately suppressed indications, but now it was too late to do anything to counter them. Of course, it was certain that the popularity of fasting would return once more someday, but for those now alive that was no consolation. What was the hunger artist to do now? The man whom thousands of people had cheered on could not display himself in show booths at small fun fairs, and the hunger artist was not only too old to take up a different profession, but was fanatically devoted to fasting more than anything else. So he said farewell to the impresario, an incomparable companion on his life's road, and let himself be hired by a large circus. In order to spare his own feelings, he didn't even look at the terms of his contract at all.

A large circus with its huge number of men, animals, and sideshows, which are constantly being let go and replenished, can use anyone at any time, even a hunger artist, provided, of course, his demands are modest. Moreover, in this particular case it was not only the hunger artist himself who was engaged, but also his old and famous name. In fact, given the characteristic nature of his art, which was not diminished by his advancing age, one could never claim that a worn-out artist, who no longer stood at the pinnacle of his ability, wanted to escape to a quiet position in the circus. On the contrary, the hunger artist declared that he could fast just as well as in earlier times—something that was entirely credible. Indeed, he even affirmed that if people would let him do what he wanted—and he was promised this without further ado— he would really now legitimately amaze the world for the first time, an assertion which, however, given the mood of the time, something the hunger artist in his enthusiasm easily overlooked, only brought smiles from the experts.

However, basically the hunger artist had also not forgotten his sense of the way things really were, and he took it as self-evident that people would not set him and his cage up as some star attraction in the middle of the arena, but would move him outside in some other readily accessible spot near the animal stalls. Huge

brightly painted signs surrounded the cage and announced what
there was to look at there. During the intervals in the main performance, when the general public pushed out towards the
menagerie in order to see the animals, they could hardly avoid
moving past the hunger artist and stopping there a moment. They
would perhaps have remained with him longer, if those pushing
up behind them in the narrow passageway, who did not understand this pause on the way to the animal stalls they wanted to
see, had not made a longer peaceful observation impossible. This
was also the reason why the hunger artist began to tremble before
these visiting hours, which he naturally used to long for as the
main purpose of his life. In the early days he could hardly wait for
the pauses in the performances. He had looked forward with
delight to the crowd pouring around him, until he became convinced only too quickly—and even the most stubborn, almost
deliberate self-deception could not hold out against the experience—that, judging by their intentions, most of these people
were, time and again without exception, only visiting the menagerie. And this view from a distance still remained his most beautiful moment. For when they had come right up to him, he immediately got an earful from the shouting and cursing of the two
steadily increasing groups, the ones who wanted to take their time
looking at the hunger artist, not with any understanding but on a
whim or from mere defiance—for him these ones were soon the
more painful—and a second group of people whose only demand
was to go straight to the animal stalls. Once the large crowds had
passed, the latecomers would arrive, and although there was
nothing preventing these people any more from sticking around
for as long as they wanted, they rushed past with long strides,
almost without a sideways glance, to get to the animals in time.
And it was an all-too-rare stroke of luck when the father of a family came by with his children, pointed his finger at the hunger
artist, gave a detailed explanation about what was going on here,
and talked of earlier years, when he had been present at similar
but incomparably more magnificent performances, and then the
children, because they had been inadequately prepared at school
and in life, always stood around still uncomprehendingly. What

69

was fasting to them? But nonetheless the brightness of the look in their searching eyes revealed something of new and more gracious times coming. Perhaps, the hunger artist said to himself sometimes, everything would be a little better if his location were not quite so near the animal stalls. That way it would be easy for people to make their choice, to say nothing of the fact that he was very upset and constantly depressed by the stink from the stalls, the animals' commotion at night, the pieces of raw meat dragged past him for the carnivorous beasts, and the roars at feeding time. But he did not dare to approach the administration about it. In any case, he had the animals to thank for the crowds of visitors among whom, now and then, there could also be one destined for him. And who knew where they would hide him if he wished to remind them of his existence and, along with that, of the fact that, strictly speaking, he was only an obstacle on the way to the menagerie?

A small obstacle, at any rate, a constantly diminishing obstacle. People became accustomed to thinking it strange that in these times they would want to pay attention to a hunger artist, and with this habitual awareness the judgment on him was pronounced. He might fast as well as he could—and he did—but nothing could save him any more. People went straight past him. Try to explain the art of fasting to anyone! If someone doesn't feel it, then he cannot be made to understand it. The beautiful signs became dirty and illegible. People tore them down, and no one thought of replacing them. The small table with the number of days the fasting had lasted, which early on had been carefully renewed every day, remained unchanged for a long time, for after the first weeks the staff grew tired of even this small task. And so the hunger artist kept fasting on and on, as he once had dreamed about in earlier times, and he had no difficulty at all managing to achieve what he had predicted back then, but no one was counting the days—no one, not even the hunger artist himself, knew how great his achievement was by this point, and his heart grew heavy. And when once in a while a person strolling past stood there making fun of the old number and talking of a swindle, that was in a sense the stupidest lie which indifference and innate maliciousness could invent, for the hunger artist was not being deceptive—he was working honestly—but the world was cheating him of his reward.

Many days went by once more, and this, too, came to an end. Finally the cage caught the attention of a supervisor, and he asked the attendant why they had left this perfectly useful cage standing here unused with rotting straw inside. Nobody knew, until one man, with the help of the table with the number on it, remembered the hunger artist. They pushed the straw around with poles and found the hunger artist in there. "Are you still fasting?" the supervisor asked. "When are you finally going to stop?" "Forgive me everything," whispered the hunger artist. Only the supervisor, who was pressing his ear up against the cage, understood him. "Certainly," said the supervisor, tapping his forehead with his finger in order to indicate to the staff the state the hunger artist was in, "we forgive you." "I always wanted you to admire my fasting," said the hunger artist. "But we do admire it," said the supervisor obligingly. "But you shouldn't admire it," said the hunger artist. "Well then, we don't admire it," said the supervisor, "but why shouldn't we admire it?" "Because I had to fast. I can't do anything else," said the hunger artist. "Just look at you," said the supervisor, "why can't you do anything else?" "Because," said the hunger artist, lifting his head a little and, with his lips pursed as if for a kiss, speaking right into the supervisor's ear so that he wouldn't miss anything, "because I couldn't find a food which tasted good to me. If I had found that, believe me, I would not have made a spectacle of myself and would have eaten to my heart's content, like you and everyone else." Those were his last words, but in his failing eyes there was still the firm, if no longer proud, conviction that he was continuing to fast.

"All right, tidy this up now," said the supervisor. And they buried the hunger artist along with the straw. But in his cage they put a young panther. Even for a person with the dullest mind it was clearly refreshing to see this wild animal prowling around in this cage, which had been dreary for such a long time. It lacked nothing. Without thinking about it for any length of time, the guards brought the animal food whose taste it enjoyed. It never seemed once to miss its freedom. This noble body, equipped with everything necessary, almost to the point of bursting, even appeared to carry freedom around with it. That seem to be located somewhere or other in its teeth, and its joy in living came with such strong passion from its throat that it was not easy for spectators to keep watching. But they controlled themselves, kept pressing around the cage, and had no desire at all to move on.

IN THE PENAL COLONY[1]

"It's a remarkable apparatus," said the Officer to the Explorer and gazed with a certain look of admiration at the device, with which he was, of course, thoroughly familiar. It appeared that the Traveller had responded to the invitation of the Commandant only out of politeness, when he had been asked to attend the execution of a soldier condemned for disobeying and insulting his superior. Interest in this execution was not really very high even in the penal colony itself. At least, here in the small, deep, sandy valley, closed in on all sides by barren slopes, apart from the Officer and the Traveller there were present only the Condemned, a vacant-looking man with a broad mouth and dilapidated hair and face, and the Soldier, who held the heavy chain to which were connected the small chains which bound the Condemned Man by his feet and wrist bones, as well as by his neck, and which were also linked to each other by connecting chains. The Condemned Man, incidentally, had an expression of such dog-like resignation that it looked as if one could set him free to roam around the slopes and would only have to whistle at the start of the execution for him to return.

The Traveller had little interest in the apparatus and walked back and forth behind the Condemned Man, almost visibly indifferent, while the Officer took care of the final preparations. Sometimes he crawled under the apparatus, which was built deep into the earth, and sometimes he climbed up a ladder to inspect the upper parts. These were jobs which really could have been left to a mechanic, but the Officer carried them out with great enthusiasm, maybe because he was particularly fond of this apparatus or maybe because there was some other reason why the work could not be entrusted to anyone else. "It's all ready now!" he finally cried and climbed back down the ladder. He was unusually tired, breathing with his mouth wide open, and he had pushed two fine lady's handkerchiefs under the collar of his uniform at the back. "These uniforms are really too heavy for the tropics," the Traveller said, instead of asking some questions about the apparatus, as the

[1]First published in 1919 in Leipzig.

Officer had expected. "That's true," said the Officer. He washed the oil and grease from his dirty hands in a bucket of water standing ready, "But they mean home, and we don't want to lose our homeland." "Now, have a look at this apparatus," he added immediately, drying his hands with a towel and at the same time pointing to the apparatus. "Up to this point I still had to do some work by hand, but from now on the apparatus works entirely on its own." The Traveller nodded and followed the Officer. The latter tried to protect himself against all eventualities by saying, "Of course, breakdowns do happen. I really hope none will occur today, but we must be prepared for them. The apparatus is supposed to keep going for twelve hours without interruption. But if any breakdowns occur, they are only very minor and will be dealt with right away."

"Don't you want to sit down?" he asked finally. He pulled out a chair from a pile of cane chairs and offered it to the Traveller. The latter could not refuse. He was now sitting on the edge of a pit, into which he cast a fleeting glance. It was not very deep. On one side of the hole the piled earth was heaped up into a wall; on the other side stood the apparatus. "I don't know," the Officer said, "whether the Commandant has already explained the apparatus to you." The Traveller made a vague gesture with his hand. That was good enough for the Officer, for now he could explain the apparatus himself. "This apparatus," he said, grasping a connecting rod and leaning against it, "is our previous Commandant's invention. I also worked with him on the very first tests and took part in all the work right up to its completion. However, the credit for the invention belongs entirely to him alone. Have you heard of our previous Commandant? No? Well, I'm not claiming too much when I say that the organization of the entire penal colony is his work. We, his friends, already knew at the time of his death that the administration of the colony was so self-contained that even if his successor had a thousand new plans in mind, he would not be able to alter anything of the old plan, at least not for several years. And our prediction has held. The New Commandant has had to recognize that. It's a shame that you didn't know the previous

Commandant!" However," the Officer said, interrupting himself, "I'm chattering, and his apparatus stands here in front of us. As you see, it consists of three parts. With the passage of time certain popular names have been developed for each of these parts. The one underneath is called the Bed, the upper one is called the Inscriber, and here in the middle, this moving part is called the Harrow." "The Harrow?" the Traveller asked. He had not been listening with full attention. The sun was excessively strong, trapped in the shadowless valley, and one could hardly collect one's thoughts. So the Officer appeared to him all the more admirable in his tight tunic weighed down with epaulettes and festooned with braid, ready to go on parade, as he explained the matter so eagerly and, in addition, while he was talking, still kept adjusting screws here and there with a screwdriver. The Soldier appeared to be in a state similar to the Traveller. He had wound the Condemned Man's chain around both his wrists and was supporting himself with his hand on his weapon, letting his head hang backward, not bothering about anything. The Traveller was not surprised at that, for the Officer spoke French, and clearly neither the Soldier nor the Condemned Man understood the language. So it was certainly all the more striking that the Condemned Man, in spite of that, did what he could to follow the Officer's explanations. With a sort of sleepy persistence he kept directing his gaze to the place where the Officer had just pointed, and when a question from the Traveller interrupted the Officer, the Condemned Man looked at the Traveller, too, just as the Officer was doing.

"Yes, the Harrow," said the Officer. "The name fits. The needles are arranged as in a harrow, and the whole thing is driven like a harrow, although it stays in one place and is, in principle, much more artistic. Anyway, you'll understand in a moment. The condemned is laid out here on the Bed. I'll describe the apparatus first and only then let the procedure go to work. That way you'll be able to follow it better. Also a sprocket in the Inscriber is excessively worn. It really squeaks. When it's in motion one can hardly make oneself understood. Unfortunately replacement parts are difficult to come by in this place. So, here is the Bed, as I said. The whole thing is completely covered with a layer of cotton wool, the purpose of which you'll find out in a moment. The condemned man is laid out on his stomach on this cotton wool—naked, of course. There are straps for the hands here, for the feet here, and for the throat here, to tie him in securely. At the head of the Bed here, where the man, as I have mentioned, first lies face down, is this small protruding lump of felt, which can easily be adjusted so that it presses right into the man's mouth. Its purpose is to prevent him screaming and biting his tongue to pieces. Of course, the man has to let the felt in his mouth—otherwise the straps around his throat will break his neck." "That's cotton wool?" asked the Traveller and bent down. "Yes, it is," said the Officer smiling, "feel it for yourself." He took the Traveller's hand and led him over to the Bed. "It's a specially prepared cotton wool. That's why it looks so unrecognizable. I'll get around to mentioning its purpose in a moment." The Traveller was already being won over a little to the apparatus. With his hand over his eyes to protect them from the sun, he looked up at the height of the apparatus. It was a massive construction. The Bed and the Inscriber were the same size and looked like two dark chests. The Inscriber was set about two metres above the Bed, and the two were joined together at the corners by four brass rods, which almost reflected rays from the sun. The Harrow hung between the chests on a band of steel.

The Officer had hardly noticed the earlier indifference of the Traveller, but he did have a sense now of how the latter's interest was being aroused now. So he paused in his explanation in order to allow the Traveller time to observe the apparatus undisturbed. The Condemned Man imitated the Traveller, but since he could not put his hand over his eyes, he blinked upward with his eyes uncovered.

"So now the man is lying down," said the Traveller. He leaned back in his chair and crossed his legs.

"Yes," said the Officer. He pushed his cap back a little and ran his hand over his hot face. "Now, listen. Both the Bed and the Inscriber have their own electric batteries. The Bed needs them for itself, and the Inscriber for the Harrow. As soon as the man is strapped in securely, the Bed is set in motion. It quivers with tiny, very rapid oscillations from side to side and up and down simultaneously. You will have seen similar devices in mental hospitals. Only with our Bed all movements are precisely calibrated, for they must be meticulously coordinated with the movements of the Harrow. But it's the Harrow which has the job of actually carrying out the sentence."

"What is the sentence?" the Traveller asked. "You don't even know that?" asked the Officer in astonishment and bit his lip. "Forgive me if my explanations are perhaps confused. I really do beg your pardon. Previously it was the Commandant's habit to provide such explanations. But the New Commandant has excused himself from this honourable duty. However, the fact that with such an eminent visitor"—the Traveller tried to deflect the honour with both hands, but the Officer insisted on the expression—"that with such an eminent visitor he didn't even once make him aware of the form of our sentencing is yet again something new, which . . ." He had a curse on his lips, but controlled himself and said merely: "I was not informed about it. It's not my fault. In any case, I am certainly the person best able to explain our style of sentencing, for here I am carrying"—he patted his breast pocket—"the relevant diagrams drawn by the previous Commandant."

"Diagrams made by the Commandant himself?" asked the Traveller. "Then was he in his own person a combination of everything? Was he soldier, judge, engineer, chemist, and draftsman?"

"He was indeed," said the Officer, nodding his head with a fixed and thoughtful expression. Then he looked at his hands, examining them. They didn't seem to him clean enough to handle the diagrams. So he went to the bucket and washed them again. Then he pulled out a small leather folder and said, "Our sentence does not sound severe. The law which a condemned man has violated

is inscribed on his body with the Harrow. This Condemned Man,
for example," and the Officer pointed to the man, "will have
inscribed on his body, 'Honour your superiors!'"

The Traveller had a quick look at the man. When the Officer was
pointing at him, the man kept his head down and appeared to be
directing all his energy into listening in order to learn something.
But the movements of his pouting lips, which were pressed close
together, showed clearly that he was incapable of understanding
anything. The Traveller wanted to raise various questions, but,
after looking at the Condemned Man, he merely asked, "Does he
know his sentence?" "No," said the Officer. He wished to get on
with his explanation right away, but the Traveller interrupted
him: "He doesn't know his own sentence?" "No," said the Officer
once more. He then paused for a moment, as if he was requesting
from the Traveller a more detailed reason for his question, and
said, "It would be useless to give him that information. He experiences it on his own body." The Traveller really wanted to keep
quiet at this point, but he felt how the Condemned Man was gazing at him—he seemed to be asking whether he could approve of
the process the Officer had described. So the Traveller, who had
up to this point been leaning back, bent forward again and kept
up his questions, "But does he nonetheless have some general idea
that he's been condemned?" "Not that either," said the Officer,
and he smiled at the Traveller, as if he was still waiting for some
strange revelations from him. "No?" said the Traveller, wiping his
forehead, "So the man does not yet know even at this point how
his defence was received?" "He has had no opportunity to defend
himself," said the Officer and looked away, as if he was talking to
himself and did not wish to embarrass the Traveller with an
explanation of matters so self-evident to him. "But he must have
had a chance to defend himself," said the Traveller and stood up
from his chair.

The Officer recognized that he was in danger of having his explanation of the apparatus held up for a long time. So he went to the
Traveller, took him by the arm, pointed with his hand at the Condemned Man, who stood there stiffly now that the attention was

so clearly directed at him—the Soldier was also pulling on his chain—and said, "The matter stands like this. Here in the penal colony I have been appointed judge. In spite of my youth. For I stood at the side of our previous Commandant in all matters of punishment, and I also know the most about the apparatus. The basic principle I use for my decisions is this: Guilt is always beyond a doubt. Other courts could not follow this principle, for they are made up of many heads and, in addition, have even higher courts above them. But that is not the case here, or at least it was not that way with the previous Commandant. It's true the New Commandant has already shown a desire to get mixed up in my court, but I've succeeded so far in fending him off. And I'll continue to be successful. You wanted this case explained. It's so simple—just like all of them. This morning a captain laid a charge that this man, who is assigned to him as a servant and who sleeps before his door, had been sleeping on duty. For his duty is to stand up every time the clock strikes the hour and salute in front of the captain's door. That's certainly not a difficult duty—and it's necessary, since he is supposed to remain fresh both for guarding and for service. Yesterday night the captain wanted to check whether his servant was fulfilling his duty. He opened the door on the stroke of two and found him curled up asleep. He got his horsewhip and hit him across the face. Now, instead of standing up and begging for forgiveness, the man grabbed his master by the legs, shook him, and cried out, 'Throw away that whip or I'll eat you up.' Those are the facts. The captain came to me an hour ago. I wrote up his statement and right after that the sentence. Then I had the man chained up. It was all very simple. If I had first summoned the man and interrogated him, the result would have been confusion. He would have lied, and if I had been successful in refuting his lies, he would have replaced them with new lies, and so forth. But now I have him, and I won't release him again. Now, does that clarify everything? But time is passing. We should be starting the execution already, and I haven't finished explaining the apparatus yet." He urged the Traveller to sit down in his chair, moved to the apparatus again, and started, "As you see, the shape of the Harrow corresponds to the shape of a man. This is the harrow for the upper body, and here are the harrows for the legs. This small cutter is the only one designated for the head. Is that clear to you?" He leaned forward to the Traveller in a friendly way, ready to give the most comprehensive explanation.

The Traveller looked at the Harrow with a wrinkled frown. The information about the judicial procedures had not satisfied him. However, he had to tell himself that here it was a matter of a penal colony, that in this place special regulations were necessary, and that one had to give precedence to military measures right down to the last detail. Beyond that, however, he had some hopes in the New Commandant, who obviously, although slowly, was intending to introduce a new procedure which the limited understanding of this Officer could not accept. Following this train of thought, the Traveller asked, "Will the Commandant be present at the execution?" "That is not certain," said the Officer, embarrassingly affected by the sudden question, and his friendly expression made a grimace. "That is why we need to hurry up. As much as I regret the fact, I'll have to make my explanation even shorter. But tomorrow, once the apparatus is clean again—the fact that it gets so very dirty is its only fault—I could add a more detailed explanation. So now, only the most essential things. When the man is lying on the Bed and it starts quivering, the Harrow sinks onto the body. It positions itself automatically in such a way that it touches the body only lightly with the needle tips. Once the machine is set in position, this steel cable tightens up immediately into a rod. And now the performance begins. Someone who is not an initiate sees no external difference among the punishments. The Harrow seems to do its work uniformly. As it quivers, it sticks the tips of its needles into the body, which is also vibrating from the movement of the bed. Now, to enable someone to check on how the sentence is being carried out, the Harrow is made of glass. That gave rise to certain technical difficulties with fastening the needles in it securely, but after several attempts we were successful. We didn't spare any efforts. And now, as the inscription is made on the body, everyone can see through the glass. Don't you want to come closer and see the needles for yourself."

The Traveller stood slowly, moved up, and bent over the Harrow. "You see," the Officer said, "two sorts of needles in a multiple arrangement. Each long needle has a short one next to it. The long one inscribes, and the short one squirts water out to wash away the blood and keep the inscription always clear. The bloody water is then channelled here into small grooves and finally flows into these main gutters, and their outlet pipe takes it to the pit." The Officer indicated with his finger the exact path which the bloody water had to take. As he began formally to demonstrate with both hands at the mouth of the outlet pipe, in order to make his account as clear as possible, the Traveller raised his head and, feeling behind him with his hand, wanted to return to his chair. Then he saw to his horror that the Condemned Man had also, like him, accepted the Officer's invitation to inspect the arrangement of the Harrow up close. He had pulled the sleeping Soldier holding the chain a little forward and was also bending over the glass. One could see how with a confused gaze he also was looking for what the two gentlemen had just observed, but how he didn't succeed because he lacked the explanation. He leaned forward this way and that. He kept running his eyes over the glass again and again. The Traveller wanted to push him back, for what he was doing was probably punishable. But the Officer held the Traveller firmly with one hand, and with the other he took a lump of earth from the wall and threw it at the Soldier. The latter opened his eyes with a start, saw what the Condemned Man had dared to do, let his weapon fall, braced his heels in the earth, and jerked the Condemned Man back, so that he immediately collapsed. The Soldier looked down at him, as he writhed around, making his chain clink. "Stand him up," cried the Officer, for he noticed that the Condemned Man was distracting the Traveller too much. The latter was even leaning out away from the Harrow, without paying any attention to it and wanted merely to find out what was happening to the Condemned Man. "Handle him carefully," the Officer yelled again. He ran around the apparatus, personally grabbed the Condemned Man under the armpits and, with the help of the Soldier, straightened up the man, whose feet kept slipping.

"Now I know all about it," said the Traveller, as the Officer turned back to him again. "Except the most important thing," said the latter. He grabbed the Traveller by the arm and pointed up high. "There in the Inscriber is the mechanism which determines the movement of the Harrow, and this mechanism is arranged according to the diagram on which the sentence is set down. I still use the diagrams of the previous Commandant. Here they are." He pulled some pages out of the leather folder. "Unfortunately I can't hand them to you. They are the most cherished thing I possess. Sit down, and I'll show you them from this distance. Then you'll be able to see it all well." He showed the first sheet. The Traveller would have been happy to say something appreciative, but all he saw was a labyrinthine series of lines, crisscrossing each other in all sorts of ways. These covered the paper so thickly that only with difficulty could one make out the white spaces in between. "Read it," said the Officer. "I can't," said the Traveller. "But it's clear," said the Officer." "It's very elaborate," said the Traveller evasively, "but I can't decipher it." "Yes," said the Officer, smiling and putting the folder back again, "it's not calligraphy for school children. One has to read it a long time. You, too, would finally understand it clearly. Of course, it has to be a script that isn't simple. You see, it's not supposed to kill right away, but on average over a period of twelve hours. The turning point is set for the sixth hour. There must also be many, many embellishments surrounding the basic script. The essential script moves around the body only in a narrow belt. The rest of the body is reserved for decoration. Can you now appreciate the work of the Harrow and of the whole apparatus? Just look at it!" He jumped up the ladder, turned a wheel, and called down, "Watch out—move to the side!" Everything started moving. If the wheel had not squeaked, it would have been marvellous. The Officer threatened the wheel with his fist, as if he was surprised by the disturbance it created. Then he spread his arms out to the Traveller, apologized, and quickly clambered down, in order to observe the operation of the apparatus from below. Something was still not working properly, something only he noticed. He clambered up again and reached with both hands into the inside of the Inscriber. Then, in order to descend more quickly, instead of using the ladder, he slid down on one of the poles and, to make himself understandable through the noise, strained his voice to the limit as he yelled in the Traveller's ear, "Do you understand the process? The Harrow is starting to write. When it's finished with the first part of the script on the man's back, the layer of cotton wool rolls and turns the body slowly onto its side to give the Harrow a new area. Meanwhile those parts lacerated by the inscription are lying on the cotton wool which, because it has been specially treated, immediately stops the bleeding and prepares the script for a further deepening. Here, as the body continues to rotate, prongs on the edge of the Harrow then pull the cotton wool from the wounds, throw it into the pit, and the Harrow goes to work again. In this way it keeps making the inscription deeper for twelve hours. For the first six hours the condemned man goes on living almost as before. He suffers nothing but pain. After two hours, the felt is removed, for at that point the man has no more energy for screaming. Here at the head of the Bed warm rice pudding is put in this electrically heated bowl. From this the man, if he feels like it, can help himself to what he can lap up with his tongue. No one passes up this opportunity. I don't know of a single one, and I have had a lot of experience. He first loses his pleasure in eating around the sixth hour. I usually kneel down at this point and observe the phenomenon. The man rarely swallows the last bit. He merely turns it around in his mouth and spits it into the pit. When he does that, I have to lean aside or else he'll get me in the face. But how quiet the man becomes around the sixth hour! The most stupid of them begins to understand. It starts around the eyes and spreads out from there. A look that could tempt one to lie down with him under the Harrow. Nothing else happens. The man simply begins to decipher the inscription. He purses his lips, as if he is listening. You've seen that it is not easy to figure out the inscription with your eyes, but our man deciphers it with his wounds. True, it takes a lot of work. It requires six hours to complete. But then the Harrow spits all of him out and throws him into the pit, where he splashes down into the bloody water and cotton wool. Then the judgment is over, and we, the Soldier and I, quickly bury him."

The Traveller had leaned his ear towards the Officer and, with his hands in his coat pockets, was observing the machine at work. The Condemned Man was also watching, but without understanding. He bent forward a little and followed the moving needles, as the Soldier, after a signal from the Officer, cut through the back of his shirt and trousers with a knife, so that they fell off the Condemned Man. He wanted to grab the falling garments to cover his bare flesh, but the Soldier held him up high and shook the last rags from him. The Officer turned the machine off, and in the silence which then ensued the Condemned Man was laid out under the Harrow. The chains were taken off and the straps fastened in their place. For the Condemned Man it seemed at first glance to signify almost a relief. And now the Harrow sunk down a stage lower still, for he was a thin man. As the needle tips touched him, a shudder went over his skin. While the Soldier was busy with the right hand, the Condemned Man stretched out his left, with no sense of its direction. But it was pointing to where the Traveller was standing. The Officer kept looking at the Traveller from the side, without taking his eyes off him, as if he was trying to read from his face the impression he was getting of the execution, which he had now explained to him, at least superficially.

The strap meant to hold the wrist ripped off. The Soldier probably had pulled on it too hard. The Soldier showed the Officer the torn-off piece of strap, wanting him to help. So the Officer went over to him and said, with his face turned towards the Traveller, "The machine is very complicated. Now and then something has to tear or break. One shouldn't let that detract from one's overall opinion. Anyway, we have an immediate replacement for the strap. I'll use a chain—even though that will affect the sensitivity of the oscillations for the right arm." And while he put the chain in place, he still kept talking, "Our resources for maintaining the machine are very limited at the moment. Under the previous Commandant, I had free access to a cash box specially set aside exclusively for this purpose. There was a storeroom here in which all possible replacement parts were kept. I admit I made almost extravagant use of it. I mean earlier, not now, as the New Commandant claims. For him everything serves only as a pretext to fight against the old arrangements. Now he keeps the cash box for machinery under his own control, and if I ask him for a new strap, he demands the torn one as a piece of evidence, the new one doesn't arrive for ten days, and then it's an inferior brand, of not much use to me. But how I am supposed to get the machine to work in the meantime without a strap—no one's concerned about that."

The Traveller thought about the situation: it is always questionable to intervene decisively in strange circumstances. He was neither a citizen of the penal colony nor a citizen of the state to which it belonged. If he wanted to condemn this execution or even hinder it, people could say to him: You are a foreigner—keep quiet. He would have nothing in response to that, but could only add that he did not understand what he was doing on this occasion, for the purpose of his traveling was merely to observe and not to alter other people's judicial systems in any way. True, at this point the way things were turning out it was very tempting. The injustice of the process and the inhumanity of the execution were beyond doubt. No one could assume that the Traveller was acting out of any sense of his own self-interest, for the Condemned Man was a stranger to him, not a countryman and not someone who invited sympathy in any way. The Traveller himself had letters of reference from high officials and had been welcomed here with great courtesy. The fact that he had been invited to this execution even seemed to indicate that people were asking for his judgment of this court. This was all the more likely since the Commandant, as he had now had heard only too clearly, was no supporter of this process and maintained an almost hostile relationship with the Officer.

Then the Traveller heard a cry of rage from the Officer. He had just shoved the stub of felt in the Condemned Man's mouth, not without difficulty, when the Condemned Man, overcome by an irresistible nausea, shut his eyes and threw up. The Officer quickly yanked him up off the stump and wanted to turn his head aside toward the pit. But it was too late. The vomit was already flowing down onto the machine. "This is all the Commandant's fault!" cried the Officer and mindlessly rattled the brass rods at the front. "My machine's as filthy as a pigsty." With trembling hands he indicated to the Traveller what had happened. "Haven't I spent hours trying to make the Commandant understand that a day before the execution there should be no more food served? But the new, lenient administration has a different opinion. Before the man is led away, the Commandant's women cram sugary things down his throat. His whole life he's fed himself on stinking fish, and now he has to eat sweets! But that would be all right—I'd have no objections—but why don't they get a new felt, the way I've been asking him for three months now? How can anyone take this felt into his mouth without feeling disgusted—something that more than a hundred men have sucked and bitten on it as they were dying?"

The Condemned Man had laid his head down and appeared peaceful. The Soldier was busy cleaning up the machine with the Condemned Man's shirt. The Officer went up to the Traveller, who, feeling some premonition, took a step backwards. But the Officer grasped him by the hand and pulled him aside. "I want to speak a few words to you in confidence," he said. "May I do that?" "Of course," said the Traveller and listened with his eyes lowered.

"This process and this execution, which you now have an opportunity to admire, have at present no more open supporters in our colony. I am its single defender and at the same time the single advocate for the legacy of the Old Commandant. I can no longer think about a more extensive organization of the process—I'm using all my powers to maintain what there is at present. When the Old Commandant was alive, the colony was full of his supporters. I have something of the Old Commandant's persuasiveness, but I completely lack his power, and as a result the supporters have gone into hiding. There are still a lot of them, but no one admits to it. If you go into a tea house today—that is to say, on a day of execution—and keep your ears open, perhaps you'll hear nothing but ambiguous remarks. They are all supporters, but under the present Commandant, considering his present views, they are totally useless to me. And now I'm asking you: Should such a life's work," he pointed to the machine, "come to nothing because of this Commandant and the women influencing him? Should people let that happen? Even if one is only a foreigner on our island for a couple of days? But there is no time to lose. People are already preparing something against my judicial proceedings. Discussions are already taking place in the Commandant's headquarters, to which I am not invited. Even your visit today seems to me typical of the whole situation. People are cowards and send you out—a foreigner. You should have seen the executions in earlier days! The entire valley was overflowing with people, even a day before the execution. They all came merely to watch. Early in the morning the Commandant appeared with his women. Fanfares woke up the entire campsite. I delivered the news that everything was ready. The whole society—and every high official had to attend—arranged itself around the machine. This pile of cane chairs is a sorry left over from that time. The machine was freshly cleaned and glowed. For almost every execution I had new replacement parts. In front of hundreds of eyes—all the spectators stood on tip toe right up to the hills there—the condemned man was laid down under the Harrow by the Commandant himself. What nowadays has to be done by a common soldier was then my work as the senior judge, and it was an honour for me. And then the execution began! No discordant note disturbed the work of the machine. Many people did not look any more at all, but lay down with closed eyes in the sand. They all knew: now justice was being carried out. In the silence people heard nothing but the groans of the condemned man, muffled by the felt. These days the machine no longer manages to squeeze out of the condemned man a groan stronger than the felt is capable of smothering. But back then the needles which made the inscription dripped a caustic liquid which today we are not permitted to use any more. Well, then came the sixth hour! It was impossible to grant all the requests people made to be allowed to watch from up close. The Commandant, in his wisdom, arranged that the children should be taken care of before all the rest. Naturally, I was always allowed to stand close by, because of my official position. Often I crouched down there with two small children in my arms, on my right and left. How we all took in the expression of transfiguration on the martyred face! How we held our cheeks in the glow of this justice, finally attained and already passing away! What times we had, my friend!" The Officer had obviously forgotten who was standing in front of him. He had put his arm around the Traveller and laid his head on his shoulder. The Traveller was extremely embarrassed. Impatiently he looked away over the Officer's head. The Soldier had ended his task of cleaning and had just shaken some rice pudding into the bowl from a tin. No sooner had the Condemned Man, who seemed to have fully recovered already, noticed this than his tongue began to lick at the pudding. The Soldier kept pushing him away, for the pudding was probably meant for a later time, but in any case it was not proper for the Soldier to reach in and grab some food with his dirty hands and eat it in front of the famished Condemned Man.

The Officer quickly collected himself. "I didn't want to upset you in any way," he said. "I know it is impossible to make someone understand those days now. Besides, the machine still works and operates on its own. It operates on its own even when it is standing alone in this valley. And at the end, the body still keeps falling in that incredibly soft flight into the pit, even if hundreds of people are not gathered like flies around the hole the way they used to be. Back then we had to erect a strong railing around the pit. It was pulled out long ago."

The Traveller wanted to turn his face away from the Officer and looked aimlessly around him. The Officer thought he was looking at the wasteland of the valley. So he grabbed his hands, turned him around in order to catch his gaze, and asked, "Do you see the shame of it?"

But the Traveller said nothing. The Officer left him alone for a while. With his legs apart and his hands on his hips, the Officer stood still and looked at the ground. Then he smiled at the Traveller cheerfully and said, "Yesterday I was nearby when the Com-

mandant invited you. I heard the invitation. I know the Commandant. I understood right away what he intended with his invitation. Although his power might be sufficiently great to take action
against me, he doesn't yet dare to. But my guess is that with you
he is exposing me to the judgment of a respected foreigner. He
calculates things with care. You are now in your second day on
the island. You didn't know the Old Commandant and his way of
thinking. You are biased in your European way of seeing things.
Perhaps you are fundamentally opposed to the death penalty in
general and to this kind of mechanical style of execution in particular. Moreover, you see how the execution is a sad procedure,
without any public participation, using a machine which is
already somewhat damaged. Now, if we take all this together (so
the Commandant thinks) surely one could easily imagine that that
you would not consider my procedure appropriate? And if you
didn't consider it right, you wouldn't keep quiet about it—I'm still
speaking the mind of the Commandant—for you no doubt have
faith that your tried-and-true convictions are correct. It's true that
you have seen many peculiar things among many peoples and
have learned to respect them. Thus, you will probably not speak
out against the procedure with your full power, as you would perhaps in your own homeland. But the Commandant doesn't really
need that. A casual word, merely a careless remark, is enough. It
doesn't have to match your convictions at all, so long as it apparently corresponds to his wishes. I'm certain he will use all his
shrewdness to interrogate you. And his women will sit around in a
circle and perk up their ears. You will say something like, 'Among
us the judicial procedures are different,' or 'With us the accused is
questioned before the verdict,' or 'With us the accused hears the
judgment' or 'With us there are punishments other than the death
penalty' or 'With us there was torture only in the Middle Ages.'
For you all these observations appear as correct as they are self-
evident—innocent remarks which do not impugn my procedure.
But how will the Commandant take them? I see him, our excellent
Commandant—the way he immediately pushes his stool aside and
hurries out onto the balcony—I see his women, how they stream
after him. I hear his voice—the women call it a thunder voice.

And now he's speaking: 'A great Western explorer who has been commissioned to inspect judicial procedures in all countries has just said that our process based on old customs is inhuman. After this verdict of such a personality it is, of course, no longer possible for me to tolerate this procedure. So from this day on I am ordering . . . and so forth.' You want to intervene—you didn't say what he is reporting—you didn't call my procedure inhuman; by contrast, in keeping with your deep insight, you consider it the most humane and most worthy of human beings. You also admire this machinery. But it is too late. You don't even go onto the balcony, which is already filled with women. You want to attract attention. You want to cry out. But a lady's hand is covering your mouth, and I and the Old Commandant's work are lost."

The Traveller had to suppress a smile. So the work which he had considered so difficult was easy. He said evasively, "You're exaggerating my influence. The Commandant has read my letters of recommendation. He knows that I am no expert in judicial processes. If I were to express an opinion, it would be that of a lay person, no more significant than the opinion of anyone else, and in any case far less significant than the opinion of the Commandant, who, as I understand it, has very extensive powers in this penal colony. If his views of this procedure are as definite as you think they are, then I'm afraid the time has surely come for this procedure to end, without any need for my humble assistance."

Did the Officer understand by now? No, he did not yet grasp it. He shook his head vigorously, briefly looked back at the Condemned Man and the Soldier, who both flinched and stopped eating the rice, went up really close up to the Traveller, without looking into his face, but gazing at parts of his jacket, and said more gently than before: "You don't know the Commandant. Where he and all of us are concerned you are—forgive the expression—to a certain extent innocent. Your influence, believe me, cannot be overestimated. In fact, I was blissfully happy when I heard that you were to be present at the execution by yourself. This arrangement of the Commandant was aimed at me, but now I'm turning it to my advantage. Without being distracted by false insinuations and disparaging looks—which could not have been avoided with a greater number of participants at the execution— you have listened to my explanation, looked at the machine, and are now about to view the execution. Your verdict is no doubt already fixed. If some small uncertainties still remain, witnessing the execution will remove them. And now I'm asking you—help me against the Commandant!"

The Traveller did not let him go on talking. "How can I do that?" he cried. "It's totally impossible. I can help you as little as I can harm you."

"You could do it," said the Officer. With some apprehension the Traveller observed that the Officer was clenching his fists. "You could do it," repeated the Officer, even more emphatically. "I have a plan which must succeed. You think your influence is insufficient. I know it will be enough. But assuming you're right, doesn't saving this procedure require one to try everything, even those methods which may possibly be inadequate? So listen to my plan. To carry it out, it's necessary, above all, for you to keep as quiet as possible today in the colony about your verdict on this procedure. Unless someone asks you directly, you should not express any view whatsoever. But what you do say must be short and vague. People should notice that it has become difficult for you to speak about the subject, that you feel bitter, that, if you were to speak openly, you'd have to burst out cursing on the spot. I'm not asking you to lie, not at all. You should give only brief answers—something like, 'Yes, I've seen the execution' or 'Yes, I've heard the full explanation.' That's all—nothing further. For that will be enough of an indication for people to observe in you a certain bitterness, even if that's not what the Commandant will think. Naturally, he will completely misunderstand the issue and interpret it in his own way. My plan is based on that. Tomorrow a large meeting of all the higher administrative officials takes place at headquarters under the chairmanship of the Commandant. He, of course, understands how to turn such meetings into a spectacle. A gallery has been built, which is always full of spectators. I'm compelled to take part in the discussions, though they make me shiver with disgust. In any case, you will certainly be invited to the meeting. If you follow my plan today and behave accordingly, the invitation will become an emphatic request. But should you for some inexplicable reason still not be invited, you must make sure you request an invitation. Then you'll receive one without question. Now, tomorrow you are sitting with the women in the Commandant's box. With frequent upward glances he reassures himself that you are there. After various trivial and ridiculous agenda items designed only for the spectators—mostly harbour construction, always harbour construction!—the judicial process also comes up for discussion. If it's not raised by the Commandant himself or does not occur soon enough, I'll make sure that it comes up. I'll stand up and report the news of today's execution. Really briefly—just this announcement. True, such a report is not customary there; however, I'll do it, nonetheless. The Commandant thanks me, as always, with a friendly smile. And now he cannot restrain himself. He seizes this excellent opportunity. 'The report of the execution,' he'll say, or something like that, 'has just been given. I would like to add to this report only the fact that this particular execution was attended by the great explorer whose visit confers such extraordinary honour on our colony, as you all know. Even the significance of our meeting today has been increased by his presence. Do we not now wish to ask this great explorer for his appraisal of the execution based on old customs and of the process which preceded it?' Of course, there is the noise of applause everywhere, universal agreement. And I'm louder than anyone. The Commandant bows before you and says, 'Then in everyone's name, I'm putting the question to you.' And now you step up to the railing. Place your hands where everyone can see them. Otherwise the ladies will grab them and play with your fingers. And now finally come your remarks. I don't know how I'll bear the tense moments up to that point. In your speech you mustn't hold back. Let truth resound. Lean over the railing and shout it out—yes, yes, roar your opinion at the Commandant, your unshakeable opinion. But perhaps you don't want to do that. It doesn't suit your character. Perhaps in your homeland people behave differently in such situations. That's all right. That's perfectly satisfactory. Don't stand up at all. Just say a couple of words. Whisper them so that only the officials underneath you can hear them. That's enough. You don't even have to say anything at all about the lack of attendance at the execution or about the squeaky wheel, the torn strap, the disgusting felt. No. I'll take over all further details, and, believe me, if my speech doesn't chase him out of the room, it will force him to his knees, so he'll have to admit it: 'Old Commandant, I bow down before you.' That's my plan. Do you want to help me carry it out? But, of course, you want to. More than that—you have to." And the Officer gripped the Traveller by both arms and looked at him, breathing heavily into his face. He had yelled the last sentences so loudly that even the Soldier and the Condemned Man were paying attention. Although they couldn't understand a thing, they stopped eating and looked over at the Traveller, still chewing.

From the very start the Traveller had had no doubts about the answer he must give. He had experienced too much in his life to be able to waver here. Basically he was honest and unafraid. Still, with the Soldier and the Condemned Man looking at him, he hesitated a moment. But finally he said, as he had to, "No." The Officer's eyes blinked several times, but he did not take his eyes off the Traveller. "Would you like an explanation," asked the Traveller. The Officer nodded dumbly. "I am opposed to this procedure," said the Traveller. "Even before you took me into your confidence—and, of course, I will never abuse your confidence under any circumstances—I was already thinking about whether I was entitled to intervene against this procedure and whether my intervention could have even a small chance of success. And if that was the case, it was clear to me whom I had to turn to first of all—naturally, to the Commandant. You have clarified the issue for me even more, but without reinforcing my decision in any way—quite the reverse. I find your conviction genuinely moving, even if it cannot deter me."

The Officer remained silent, turned towards the machine, grabbed one of the brass rods, and then, leaning back a little, looked up at the Inscriber, as if he was checking that everything was in order.

The Soldier and the Condemned Man seemed to have made friends with each other. The Condemned Man was making signs to the Soldier, although, given the tight straps on him, this was difficult for him to do. The Soldier was leaning into him. The Condemned Man whispered something to him, and the Soldier nodded.

The Traveller went over to the Officer and said, "You don't yet know what I'll do. Yes, I will tell the Commandant my opinion of the procedure—not in a meeting, but in private. In addition, I won't stay here long enough to be able to get called in to some meeting or other. Early tomorrow morning I leave, or at least I go on board ship."

It did not look as if the Officer had been listening. "So the process has not convinced you," he said to himself and smiled the way an old man smiles over the silliness of a child, concealing his own true thoughts behind that smile.

"Well then, it's time," he said finally and suddenly looked at the Traveller with bright eyes which contained some sort of demand, some appeal for participation. "Time for what?" asked the Traveller uneasily. But there was no answer.

"You are free," the Officer told the Condemned Man in his own language. At first the man did not believe him. "You are free now," said the Officer. For the first time the face of the Condemned Man showed signs of real life. Was it the truth? Was it only the Officer's mood, which could change? Had the foreign Traveller brought him a reprieve? What was it? That is what the man's face seemed to be asking. But not for long. Whatever the case might be, if he could he wanted to be truly free, and he began to shake back and forth, as much as the Harrow permitted.

"You're tearing my straps," cried the Officer. "Be still! We'll undo them right away." And, giving a signal to the Soldier, he set to work with him. The Condemned Man said nothing and smiled slightly to himself. At times he turned his face to the Officer on

94

the left and at times to the Soldier on the right, without ignoring the Traveller.

"Pull him out," the Officer ordered the Soldier. This process required a certain amount of care because of the Harrow. The Condemned Man already had a few small wounds on his back, thanks to his own impatience.

From this point on, however, the Officer paid no more attention to him. He went up to the Traveller, pulled out the small leather folder once more, leafed through it, finally found the sheet he was looking for, and showed it to the Traveller. "Read that," he said. "I can't," said the Traveller. "I've already told you I can't read these pages." "But take a close look at the page," said the Officer and moved up right next to the Traveller in order to read with him. When that didn't help, he raised his little finger high up over the paper, as if the page must not be touched under any circumstances, so that using this he might make the task of reading easier for the Traveller. The Traveller also made an effort so that at least he could satisfy the Officer, but it was impossible for him. At that point the Officer began to spell out the inscription, and then he read out once again the joined up letters. "'Be just!' it states," he said. "Now you can read it." The Traveller bent so low over the paper that the Officer, afraid that he might touch it, moved it further away. The Traveller didn't say anything more, but it was clear that he was still unable to read anything. "'Be just!' it says," the Officer remarked once again. "That could be," said the Traveller. "I do believe that's written there." "Good," said the Officer, at least partially satisfied. He climbed up the ladder, holding the paper. With great care he set the page in the Inscriber and appeared to rotate the gear mechanism completely around. This was very tiring work. It must have required him to deal with extremely small wheels. He had to inspect the gears so closely that sometimes the Officer's head disappeared completely into the Inscriber.

The Traveller followed this work from below without looking away. His neck grew stiff, and his eyes found the sunlight pouring down from the sky painful. The Soldier and the Condemned Man were keeping each other busy. With the tip of his bayonet the Soldier pulled out the Condemned Man's shirt and trousers which were lying in the hole. The shirt was horribly dirty, and the Condemned Man washed it in the bucket of water. When he was putting on his shirt and trousers, the Soldier and the Condemned Man had to laugh out loud, for the pieces of clothing were cut in two up the back. Perhaps the Condemned Man thought that it was his duty to amuse the Soldier. In his ripped-up clothes he circled in front of the Soldier, who crouched down on the ground, laughed, and slapped his knees. But they still restrained themselves out of consideration for the two gentlemen present.

When the Officer was finally finished up on the machine, with a smile he looked over the whole thing and all its parts once more, and this time closed the cover of the Inscriber, which had been open up to this point. He climbed down, looked into the hole and then at the Condemned Man, observed with satisfaction that his clothes had been hauled out, then went to the bucket of water to wash his hands, recognized too late that it was disgustingly dirty, and was upset that now he could not wash his hands. Finally he pushed them into the sand. This option did not satisfy him, but he had to do what he could in the circumstances. Then he stood up and began to unbutton the coat of his uniform. As he did this, the two lady's handkerchiefs, which he had pushed into the back of his collar, fell into his hands. "Here you have your handkerchiefs," he said and threw them over to the Condemned Man. And to the Traveller he said by way of an explanation, "Presents from the ladies."

In spite of the obvious speed with which he took off the coat of his uniform and then undressed himself completely, he handled each piece of clothing very carefully, even running his fingers over the silver braids on his tunic with special care and shaking a tassel into place. But in great contrast to this care, as soon he was finished handling an article of clothing, he immediately flung it angrily into the hole. The last items he had left were his short sword and its harness. He pulled the sword out of its scabbard, broke it in pieces, then gathered up everything—the pieces of the sword, the scabbard, and the harness—and threw them away so forcefully that they rattled against each other down in the pit.

Now he stood there naked. The Traveller bit his lip and said nothing. For he was aware what would happen, but he had no right to hinder the Officer in any way. If the judicial process to which the Officer clung was really so close to the point of being cancelled—possibly as a result of the intervention of the Traveller, something to which he for his part felt duty-bound—then the Officer was now acting in a completely correct manner. In his place, the Traveller would not have acted any differently.

The Soldier and the Condemned Man at first did not understand a thing. To begin with they did not look, not even once. The Condemned Man was extremely happy to get the handkerchiefs back, but he was not permitted to enjoy them very long, because the Soldier snatched them from him with a quick grab, which he had not anticipated. The Condemned Man then tried to pull the handkerchiefs out from the Soldier's belt, where he had put them for safe keeping, but the Soldier was watching carefully. So they were fighting, half in jest. Only when the Officer was fully naked did they start to pay attention. The Condemned Man especially seemed to be struck by a premonition of some sort of significant transformation. What had happened to him was now taking place with the Officer. Perhaps this time the procedure would play itself out to its conclusion. The foreign Traveller had probably given the order for it. So that was revenge. Without having suffered all the way to the end himself, nonetheless he would be completely avenged. A wide, silent laugh now appeared on his face and never went away.

The Officer, however, had turned towards the machine. If earlier on it had already become clear that he understood the machine thoroughly, one could well get alarmed now at the way he handled it and how it obeyed. He only had to bring his hand near the Harrow for it to rise and sink several times, until it had reached the correct position to make room for him. He only had to grasp

97

the Bed by the edges, and it already began to quiver. The stump of felt moved up to his mouth. One could see how the Officer really did not want to accept it, but his hesitation was only momentary—he immediately submitted and took it in. Everything was ready, except that the straps still hung down on the sides. But they were clearly unnecessary. The Officer did not have to be strapped down. When the Condemned Man saw the loose straps, he thought the execution would be incomplete unless they were fastened. He waved eagerly to the Soldier, and they ran over to strap in the Officer. The latter had already stuck out his foot to kick the crank designed to set the Inscriber in motion. Then he saw the two men coming. So he pulled his foot back and let himself be strapped in. But now he could no longer reach the crank. Neither the Soldier nor the Condemned Man would find it, and the Traveller was determined not to touch it. But that was unnecessary. Hardly were the straps attached when the machine already started working: the Bed quivered, the needles danced on his skin, and the Harrow swung up and down. The Traveller had already been staring for some time before he remembered that a wheel in the Inscriber was supposed to squeak. But everything was quiet, without the slightest audible hum.

Because of its silent working, the machine did not really attract attention. The Traveller looked over at the Soldier and the Condemned Man. The Condemned Man was the livelier of the two. Everything in the machine interested him. At times he bent down; at other times he stretched up, always pointing with his forefinger in order to show something to the Soldier. For the Traveller it was embarrassing. He was determined to remain here until the end, but he could no longer endure the sight of the two men. "Go home," he said. The Soldier might perhaps have been ready to do that, but the Condemned Man took the order as a direct punishment. With his hands folded he pleaded to be allowed to stay there. And when the Traveller shook his head and was unwilling to give in, he even knelt down. Seeing that orders were of no help here, the Traveller wanted to go over and chase the two away. Then he heard a noise from up in the Inscriber. He looked up. So was the gear wheel going out of alignment? But it was something else. The lid on the Inscriber was lifting up slowly. Then it fell completely open. The teeth of a cog wheel were exposed and lifted up. Soon the entire wheel appeared. It was as if some huge force was compressing the Inscriber, so that there was no longer sufficient room left for this wheel. The wheel rolled all the way to the edge of the Inscriber, fell down, rolled upright a bit in the sand, and then fell over and lay still. But already up on the Inscriber another gear wheel was moving upwards. Several others followed—large ones, small ones, ones hard to distinguish. With each of them the same thing happened. One kept thinking that now the Inscriber must surely be already empty, but then a new cluster with lots of parts would move up, fall down, roll in the sand, and lie still. With all this going on, the Condemned Man totally forgot the Traveller's order. The gear wheels completely delighted him. He kept wanting to grab one, and at the same time he was urging the Soldier to help him. But he kept pulling his hand back startled, for immediately another wheel followed, which, at least in its initial rolling, surprised him.

The Traveller, by contrast, was very upset. Obviously the machine was breaking up. Its quiet operation had been an illusion. He felt as if he had to look after the Officer, now that the latter could no longer look after himself. But while the falling gear wheels were claiming all his attention, he had neglected to look at the rest of the machine. However, when he now bent over the Harrow, once the last gear wheel had left the Inscriber, he had a new, even more unpleasant surprise. The Harrow was not writing but only stabbing, and the Bed was not rolling the body, but lifting it, quivering, up into the needles. The Traveller wanted to reach in to stop the whole thing, if possible. This was not the torture the Officer wished to attain; it was murder, pure and simple. He stretched out his hands. But at that point the Harrow was already moving upwards and to the side, with the skewered body—just as it did in other cases, but only in the twelfth hour. Blood flowed out in hundreds of streams, not mixed with water—the water tubes had failed to work this time, as well. Then one last thing went wrong:

the body would not come loose from the long needles. Its blood streamed out, but it hung over the pit without falling. The Harrow wanted to move back to its original position, but, as if realizing that it could not free itself of its load, it remained over the hole. "Help," the Traveller yelled out to the Soldier and the Condemned Man, and he himself grabbed the Officer's feet. He wanted to push against the feet himself and have the two others grab the Officer's head from the other side, so he could be slowly lifted off the needles. But now the two men could not make up their mind whether to come or not. The Condemned Man turned away at once. The Traveller had to go over to him and drag him to the Officer's head by force. At this point, almost against his will, he looked at the face of the corpse. It was as it had been in life. He could discover no sign of the promised transfiguration. What all the others had found in the machine, the Officer had not. His lips were pressed firmly together, his eyes were open and looked as they had when he was alive, his gaze was calm and convinced. The tip of a large iron needle had gone through his forehead.

*   *   *

As the Traveller, with the Soldier and the Condemned Man behind him, came to the first houses in the colony, the Soldier pointed to one and said, "That's the tea house."

On the ground floor of the house was a deep, low room, like a cave, with smoke-covered walls and ceiling. On the street side it was open along its full width. Although there was little difference between the tea house and the rest of the houses in the colony, which were all very dilapidated, except for the Commandant's palatial structure, the Traveller was nonetheless struck by the impression of historical memory, and he felt the power of earlier times. Followed by his companions, he walked closer inside, going between the unoccupied tables, which stood in the street in front of the tea house, and took a breath of the cool, musty air which came from inside. "The old man is buried here," said the Soldier; "a place in the cemetery was denied him by the chaplain. For a while people were undecided where they should bury him. Finally

100

they buried him here. Of course, the Officer explained none of that to you, for naturally he was the one most ashamed about it. A few times he even tried to dig up the old man at night, but he was always chased off." "Where is the grave?" asked the Traveller, who could not believe the Soldier. Instantly both men, the Soldier and the Condemned Man, ran in front of him and with hands outstretched pointed to the place where the grave was located. They led the Traveller to the back wall, where guests were sitting at a few tables. They were presumably dock workers, strong men with short, shiny, black beards. None of them wore coats, and their shirts were torn. They were poor, humiliated people. As the Traveller came closer, a few got up, leaned against the wall, and looked at him. A whisper went up around the Traveller—"It's a foreigner. He wants to look at the grave." They pushed one of the tables aside, under which there was a real grave stone. It was a simple stone, low enough for it to remain hidden under a table. It bore an inscription in very small letters. In order to read it the Traveller had to kneel down. It read, "Here rests the Old Commandant. His followers, who are now not permitted to have a name, buried him in this grave and erected this stone. There exists a prophecy that the Commandant will rise again after a certain number of years and from this house will lead his followers to a re-conquest of the colony. Have faith and wait!" When the Traveller had read it and got up, he saw the men standing around him and smiling, as if they had read the inscription with him, found it ridiculous, and were asking him to share their opinion. The Traveller acted as if he had not noticed, distributed some coins among them, waited until the table was pushed back over the grave, left the tea house, and went to the harbour.

In the tea house the Soldier and the Condemned Man had come across some people they knew who detained them. However, they must have broken free of them soon, because by the time the Traveller found himself in the middle of a long staircase which led to the boats, they were already running after him. They probably wanted to force the Traveller at the last minute to take them with him. While the Traveller was haggling at the bottom of the stairs with a sailor about his passage out to the steamer, the two men were racing down the steps in silence, for they did not dare cry out. But as they reached the bottom, the Traveller was already in the boat, and the sailor at once cast off from shore. They could still have jumped into the boat, but the Traveller picked up a heavy knotted rope from the boat bottom, threatened them with it, and thus prevented them from jumping in.

THE METAMORPHOSIS[1]

One morning, as Gregor Samsa was waking up from anxious dreams, he discovered that in his bed he had been changed into a monstrous verminous bug. He lay on his armour-hard back and saw, as he lifted his head up a little, his brown, arched abdomen divided up into rigid bow-like sections. From this height the blanket, just about ready to slide off completely, could hardly stay in place. His numerous legs, pitifully thin in comparison to the rest of his circumference, flickered helplessly before his eyes.

"What's happened to me," he thought. It was no dream. His room, a proper room for a human being, only somewhat too small, lay quietly between the four well-known walls. Above the table, on which an unpacked collection of sample cloth goods was spread out—Samsa was a travelling salesman—hung the picture which he had cut out of an illustrated magazine a little while ago and set in a pretty gilt frame. It was a picture of a woman with a fur hat and a fur boa. She sat erect there, lifting up in the direction of the viewer a solid fur muff into which her entire forearm had disappeared.

Gregor's glance then turned to the window. The dreary weather—the rain drops were falling audibly down on the metal window ledge—made him quite melancholy. "Why don't I keep sleeping for a little while longer and forget all this foolishness," he thought. But this was entirely impractical, for he was used to sleeping on his right side, but in his present state he could not get himself into this position. No matter how hard he threw himself onto his right side, he always rolled onto his back again. He must have tried it a hundred times, closing his eyes so that he would not have to see the wriggling legs, and gave up only when he began to feel a light, dull pain in his side which he had never felt before.

"O God," he thought, "what a demanding job I've chosen! Day in, day out, on the road. The stresses of selling are much greater than the actual work going on at head office, and, in addition to that, I still have to cope with the problems of travelling, the worries

[1]First published in *Die Weissßen Blätter*, October 1915.

about train connections, irregular bad food, temporary and constantly changing human relationships, which never come from the heart. To hell with it all!" He felt a slight itching on the top of his abdomen. He slowly pushed himself on his back closer to the bed post so that he could lift his head more easily, found the itchy part, which was entirely covered with small white spots—he did not know what to make of them and wanted to feel the place with a leg, but he retracted it immediately, for the contact felt like a cold shower all over him.

He slid back again into his earlier position. "This getting up early," he thought, "makes a man quite idiotic. A man must have his sleep. Other travelling salesmen live like harem women. For instance, when I come back to the inn during the course of the morning to write up the necessary orders, these gentlemen are just sitting down to breakfast. If I were to try that with my boss, I'd be thrown out on the spot. Still, who knows whether that mightn't be really good for me. If I didn't hold back for my parents' sake, I'd have quit ages ago. I would've gone to the boss and told him just what I think from the bottom of my heart. He would've fallen right off his desk! How weird it is to sit up at that desk and talk down to the employee from way up there. What's more, the boss has trouble hearing, so the employee has to step up quite close to him. Anyway, I haven't completely given up that hope yet. Once I've got together the money to pay off my parents' debt to him—that should take another five or six years—I'll do it for sure. Then I'll make the big break. In any case, right now I have to get up. My train leaves at five o'clock."

He looked over at the alarm clock ticking away by the chest of drawers. "Good God!" he thought. It was half past six, and the hands were going quietly on. It was even past the half hour, already nearly quarter to. Could the alarm have failed to ring? One saw from the bed that it was properly set for four o'clock. Certainly it had rung. Yes, but was it possible to sleep peacefully through that noise which made the furniture shake? Now, it is true he had not slept peacefully, but evidently he had slept all the more deeply. Still, what should he do now? The next train left at seven o'clock. To catch that one, he would have to go in a mad rush. The sample collection was not packed up yet, and he really did not feel particularly fresh and active. And even if he caught the train, there was no avoiding a blow-up with the boss, because the firm's errand boy would have waited for the five o'clock train and reported the news of his absence long ago. He was the boss's minion, without backbone and intelligence. Well then, what if he reported in sick? But that would be extremely embarrassing and suspicious, because during his five years' service Gregor had not been sick even once. The boss would certainly come with the doctor from the health insurance company and would reproach his parents for their lazy son and cut short all objections with the insurance doctor's comments; for him everyone was completely healthy but really lazy about work. And besides, would the doctor in this case be totally wrong? Apart from a really excessive drowsiness after the long sleep, Gregor, in fact, felt quite well and even had a really strong appetite.

As he was thinking all this over in the greatest haste, without being able to make the decision to get out of bed—the alarm clock was indicating exactly quarter to seven—there was a cautious knock on the door by the head of the bed. "Gregor," a voice called—it was his mother—"it's quarter to seven. Don't you want to be on your way?" The soft voice! Gregor was startled when he heard his voice answering. It was clearly and unmistakably his earlier voice, but in it was intermingled, as if from below, an irrepressible, painful squeaking, which left the words positively distinct only in the first moment and distorted them in the reverberation, so that one did not know if one had heard correctly. Gregor wanted to answer in detail and explain everything, but in these circumstances he confined himself to saying, "Yes, yes, thank you mother. I'm getting up right away." Because of the wooden door the change in Gregor's voice was not really noticeable outside, so his mother calmed down with this explanation and shuffled off. However, as a result of the short conversation, the other family members became aware that Gregor was unexpectedly still at home, and already his father was knocking on one side door, weakly but with his fist. "Gregor, Gregor," he called out, "what's going on?" And, after a short while, he urged him on again in a deeper voice: "Gregor! Gregor!" At the other side door, however, his sister knocked lightly. "Gregor? Are you all right? Do you need anything?" Gregor directed answers in both directions, "I'll be ready right away." He made an effort with the most careful articulation and inserted long pauses between the individual words to remove everything remarkable from his voice. His father turned back to his breakfast. However, the sister whispered, "Gregor, open the door—I beg you." Gregor had no intention of opening the door, but congratulated himself on his precaution, acquired from travelling, of locking all doors during the night, even at home.

First he wanted to stand up quietly and undisturbed, get dressed, above all have breakfast, and only then consider further action, for—he noticed this clearly—by thinking things over in bed he would not reach a reasonable conclusion. He remembered that he had already often felt some light pain or other in bed, perhaps the result of an awkward lying position, which later, once he stood up, turned out to be purely imaginary, and he was eager to see how his present fantasies would gradually dissipate. That the change in his voice was nothing other than the onset of a real chill, an occupational illness of commercial travellers, of that he had not the slightest doubt.

It was very easy to throw aside the blanket. He needed only to push himself up a little, and it fell by itself. But to continue was difficult, particularly because he was so unusually wide. He needed arms and hands to push himself upright. Instead of these, however, he had only many small limbs, which were incessantly moving with very different motions and which, in addition, he was unable to control. If he wanted to bend one of them, then it was the first to extend itself, and if he finally succeeded doing what he wanted with this limb, in the meantime all the others, as if left free, moved around in an excessively painful agitation. "But I must not stay in bed uselessly," said Gregor to himself.

At first he wanted to get out of bed with the lower part of his body, but this lower part—which, by the way, he had not yet looked at and which he also could not picture clearly—proved itself too difficult to move. The attempt went so slowly. When, having become almost frantic, he finally hurled himself forward with all his force and without thinking, he chose his direction incorrectly, and he hit the lower bedpost hard. The violent pain he felt revealed to him that the lower part of his body was at the moment probably the most sensitive.

Thus, he tried to get his upper body out of the bed first and turned his head carefully toward the edge of the bed. He managed to do this easily, and in spite of its width and weight his body mass at last slowly followed the turning of his head. But as he finally raised his head outside the bed in the open air, he became anxious about moving forward any further in this manner, for if he allowed himself eventually to fall by this process, it would really take a miracle to prevent his head from getting injured. And at all costs he must not lose consciousness right now. He preferred to remain in bed.

However, after a similar effort, while he lay there again, sighing as before, and once again saw his small limbs fighting one another, if anything even worse than earlier, and did not see any chance of imposing quiet and order on this arbitrary movement, he told himself again that he could not possibly remain in bed and that it might be the most reasonable thing to sacrifice everything if there was even the slightest hope of getting himself out of bed in the process. At the same moment, however, he did not forget to remind himself from time to time of the fact that calm—indeed the calmest—reflection might be much better than confused decisions. At such moments, he directed his gaze as precisely as he could toward the window, but unfortunately there was little confident cheer to be had from a glance at the morning mist, which concealed even the other side of the narrow street. "It's already seven o'clock," he told himself at the latest sounds from the alarm clock, "already seven o'clock and still such a fog." And for a little while longer he lay quietly with weak breathing, as if perhaps waiting for normal and natural conditions to re-emerge out of the complete stillness.

But then he said to himself, "Before it strikes a quarter past seven, whatever happens I must be completely out of bed. Besides, by then someone from the office will arrive to inquire about me, because the office will open before seven o'clock." And he made an effort then to rock his entire body length out of the bed with a uniform motion. If he let himself fall out of the bed in this way, his head, which in the course of the fall he intended to lift up sharply, would probably remain uninjured. His back seemed to be hard; nothing would really happen to that as a result of the fall onto the carpet. His greatest reservation was a worry about the loud noise which the fall must create and which presumably would arouse, if not fright, then at least concern on the other side of all the doors. However, he had to take that chance.

As Gregor was already in the process of lifting himself half out of bed—the new method was more of a game than an effort; he needed only to rock with a series of jerks—it struck him how easy all this would be if someone were to come to his aid. Two strong people—he thought of his father and the servant girl—would have been quite sufficient. They would only have had to push their arms under his arched back to get him out of the bed, to bend down with their load, and then merely to exercise patience so that he could complete the flip onto the floor, where his diminutive legs would then, he hoped, acquire a purpose. Now, quite apart from the fact that the doors were locked, should he really call out for help? In spite of all his distress, he was unable to suppress a smile at this idea.

He had already got to the point where, by rocking more strongly, he maintained his equilibrium with difficulty, and very soon he would finally have to make a final decision, for in five minutes it would be a quarter past seven. Then there was a ring at the door of the apartment. "That's someone from the office," he told himself, and he almost froze, while his small limbs only danced around all the faster. For one moment everything remained still.

"They aren't opening," Gregor said to himself, caught up in some absurd hope. But of course then, as usual, the servant girl with her firm tread went to the door and opened it. Gregor needed to hear only the first word of the visitor's greeting to recognize immediately who it was, the manager himself. Why was Gregor the only one condemned to work in a firm where, at the slightest lapse, someone at once attracted the greatest suspicion? Were all the employees then collectively, one and all, scoundrels? Among them was there then no truly devoted person who, if he failed to use just a couple of hours in the morning for office work, would become abnormal from pangs of conscience and really be in no state to get out of bed? Was it really not enough to let an apprentice make inquiries, if such questioning was even generally necessary? Must the manager himself come, and in the process must it be demonstrated to the entire innocent family that the investigation of this suspicious circumstance could be entrusted only to the intelligence of the manager? And more as a consequence of the excited state in which this idea put Gregor than as a result of an actual decision, he swung himself with all his might out of the bed. There was a loud thud, but not a real crash. The fall was absorbed somewhat by the carpet and, in addition, his back was more elastic than Gregor had thought. For that reason the dull noise was not quite so conspicuous. But he had not held his head up with sufficient care and had hit it. He turned his head, irritated and in pain, and rubbed it on the carpet.

"Something has fallen in there," said the manager in the next room on the left. Gregor tried to imagine to himself whether anything similar to what was happening to him today could have also happened at some point to the manager. At least one had to concede the possibility of such a thing. However, as if to give a rough answer to this question, the manager now, with a squeak of his polished boots, took a few determined steps in the next room. From the neighbouring room on the right the sister was whispering to inform Gregor: "Gregor, the manager is here." "I know," said Gregor to himself. But he did not dare make his voice loud enough so that his sister could hear.

"Gregor," his father now said from the neighbouring room on the left, "Mr. Manager has come and is asking why you have not left on the early train. We don't know what we should tell him. Besides, he also wants to speak to you personally. So please open the door. He will be good enough to forgive the mess in your room." In the middle of all this, the manager called out in a friendly way, "Good morning, Mr. Samsa." "He is not well," said his mother to the manager, while his father was still talking at the door, "He is not well, believe me, Mr. Manager. Otherwise how would Gregor miss a train? The young man has nothing in his head except business. I'm almost angry that he never goes out in the evening. Right now he's been in the city eight days, but he's been at home every evening. He sits here with us at the table and reads the newspaper quietly or studies his travel schedules. It's a quite a diversion for him to busy himself with fretwork. For instance, he cut out a small frame over the course of two or three evenings. You'd be amazed how pretty it is. It's hanging right inside the room. You'll see it immediately, as soon as Gregor opens the door. Anyway, I'm happy that you're here, Mr. Manager. By ourselves, we would never have made Gregor open the door. He's so stubborn, and he's certainly not well, although he denied that this morning." "I'm coming right away," said Gregor slowly and deliberately and didn't move, so as not to lose one word of the conversation. "My dear lady, I cannot explain it to myself in any other way," said the manager; "I hope it is nothing serious. On the other hand, I must also say that we business people, luckily or unluckily, however one looks at it, very often simply have to over-come a slight indisposition for business reasons." "So can Mr. Manager come in to see you now?" asked his father impatiently and knocked once again on the door. "No," said Gregor. In the neighbouring room on the left an awkward stillness descended. In the neighbouring room on the right the sister began to sob.

Why did his sister not go to the others? She had probably just got up out of bed now and had not even started to get dressed yet. Then why was she crying? Because he was not getting up and let-ting the manager in, because he was in danger of losing his position, and because then his boss would badger his parents once again with the old demands? Those were probably unnecessary worries right now. Gregor was still here and was not thinking at all about abandoning his family. At the moment he was lying right there on the carpet, and no one who knew about his condition would have seriously demanded that he let the manager in. But Gregor would not be casually dismissed right way because of this small discourtesy, for which he would find an easy and suitable excuse later on. It seemed to Gregor that it might be far more reasonable to leave him in peace at the moment, instead of disturbing him with crying and conversation. But it was the very uncertainty which distressed the others and excused their behaviour.

"Mr. Samsa," the manager was now shouting, his voice raised, "what's the matter? You are barricading yourself there in your room, answering with only a yes and a no, are making serious and unnecessary trouble for your parents, and neglecting—I mention this only incidentally—your commercial duties in a truly unheard of manner. I am speaking here in the name of your parents and your employer, and I am requesting you in all seriousness for an immediate and clear explanation. I am amazed. I am amazed. I thought I knew you as a calm, reasonable person, and now you appear suddenly to want to start parading around in weird moods. The Chief indicated to me earlier this very day a possible explanation for your neglect—it concerned the collection of cash entrusted to you a short while ago—but in truth I almost gave him my word of honour that this explanation could not be correct. However, now I see here your unimaginable pig-headedness, and I am totally losing any desire to speak up for you in the slightest. And your position is not at all the most secure. Originally I intended to mention all this to you privately, but since you are letting me waste my time here uselessly, I don't know why the matter shouldn't come to the attention of your parents as well. Your productivity has also been very unsatisfactory recently. Of course, it's not the time of year to conduct exceptional business, we recognize that, but a time of year for conducting no business, there is no such thing at all, Mr. Samsa, and such a thing must not be permitted."

"But Mr. Manager," called Gregor, beside himself and, in his agitation, forgetting everything else, "I'm opening the door immediately, this very moment. A slight indisposition, a dizzy spell, has prevented me from getting up. I'm still lying in bed right now. But I'm quite refreshed once again. I'm in the midst of getting out of bed. Just have patience for a short moment! Things are not yet going as well as I thought. But things are all right with me. How suddenly this can overcome someone! Only yesterday evening everything was fine with me. My parents certainly know that. Actually just yesterday evening I had a small premonition. People must have seen that in me. Why have I not reported that to the office? But people always think that they'll get over sickness without having to stay at home. Mr. Manager! Take it easy on my parents! There is really no basis for the criticisms which you're now making against me. Nobody has said a word to me about that. Perhaps you have not read the latest orders which I sent in. Besides, now I'm setting out on my trip on the eight o'clock train; the few hours' rest have made me stronger. Mr. Manager, do not stay. I will be at the office in person right away. Please have the goodness to say that and to convey my respects to the Chief."

While Gregor was quickly blurting all this out, hardly aware of what he was saying, he had moved close to the chest of drawers without effort, probably as a result of the practice he had already had in bed, and now he was trying to raise himself up on it. Actually, he wanted to open the door. He really wanted to let himself be seen and to speak with the manager. He was keen to witness what the others now asking about him would say when they saw him. If they were startled, then Gregor had no more responsibility and could be calm. But if they accepted everything quietly, then he would have no reason to get excited and, if he got a move on, could really be at the station around eight o'clock. At first he slid down a few times on the smooth chest of drawers. But at last he gave himself a final swing and stood upright there. He was no longer at all aware of the pains in his lower body, no matter how they might still sting. Now he let himself fall against the back of a nearby chair, on the edge of which he braced himself with his small limbs. By doing this he gained control over himself and kept quiet, for he could now hear the manager.

"Did you understand even a single word?" the manager asked the parents, "Is he playing the fool with us?" "For God's sake," cried the mother, already in tears, "perhaps he's very ill, and we're upsetting him. Grete! Grete!" she yelled at that point. "Mother?" called the sister from the other side. They were making themselves understood through Gregor's room. "You must go to the doctor right away. Gregor is sick. Hurry to the doctor. Did you hear Gregor speak just now?" "That was an animal's voice," said the manager, remarkably quiet in comparison to the mother's cries. "Anna! Anna!" yelled the father through the hall into the kitchen, clapping his hands, "Fetch a locksmith right away!" The two young women were already running through the hall with swishing skirts—how had his sister dressed herself so quickly?— and pulled open the doors of the apartment. One could not hear the doors closing at all. They probably had left them open, as is customary in an apartment where a huge misfortune has taken place.

However, Gregor had become much calmer. All right, people did not understand his words any more, although they seemed clear enough to him, clearer than previously, perhaps because his ears had gotten used to them. But at least people now thought that things were not completely all right with him and were prepared to help him. The confidence and assurance with which the first arrangements had been carried out made him feel good. He felt himself included once again in the circle of humanity and was expecting from both the doctor and the locksmith, without differentiating between them with any real precision, splendid and surprising results. In order to get as clear a voice as possible for the critical conversation which was imminent, he coughed a little, and certainly took the trouble to do this in a really subdued way, since it was possible that even this noise sounded like something different from a human cough. He no longer trusted himself to decide any more. Meanwhile in the next room it had become really quiet. Perhaps his parents were sitting with the manager at the table whispering; perhaps they were all leaning against the door and listening.

Gregor pushed himself slowly towards the door, with the help of the easy chair, let go of it there, threw himself against the door, held himself upright against it—the balls of his tiny limbs had a little sticky stuff on them—and rested there momentarily from his exertion. Then he made an effort to turn the key in the lock with his mouth. Unfortunately it seemed that he had no real teeth. How then was he to grab hold of the key? But to make up for that his jaws were naturally very strong; with their help he managed to get the key really moving. He did not notice that he was obviously inflicting some damage on himself, for a brown fluid came out of his mouth, flowed over the key, and dripped onto the floor. "Just listen," said the manager in the next room. "He's turning the key." For Gregor that was a great encouragement. But they should all have called out to him, including his father and mother, "Come on, Gregor," they should have shouted. "Keep going, keep working on the lock!" Imagining that all his efforts were being followed with suspense, he bit down frantically on the key with all the force he could muster. As the key turned more, he danced around the lock. Now he was holding himself upright only with his mouth, and he had to hang onto the key or then press it down again with the whole weight of his body, as necessary. The quite distinct click of the lock as it finally snapped really woke Gregor up. Breathing heavily he said to himself, "So I didn't need the locksmith," and he set his head against the door handle to open the door completely.

Because he had to open the door in this way, it was already open really wide without him yet being visible. He first had to turn himself slowly around the edge of the door, very carefully, of course, if he did not want to fall awkwardly on his back right at the entrance into the room. He was still preoccupied with this difficult movement and had no time to pay attention to anything else, when he heard the manager exclaim a loud "Oh!"—it sounded like the wind whistling—and now he saw him, nearest to the door, pressing his hand against his open mouth and moving slowly back, as if an invisible constant force was pushing him away. His mother—in spite of the presence of the manager she was standing here with her hair sticking up on end, still a mess from the night—first looked at his father with her hands clasped, then went two steps towards Gregor and collapsed right in the middle of her skirts, which were spread out all around her, her face sunk on her breast, completely concealed. His father clenched his fist with a hostile expression, as if he wished to push Gregor back into his room, then looked uncertainly around the living room, covered his eyes with his hands, and cried so that his mighty breast shook.

At this point Gregor did not take one step into the room, but leaned his body from the inside against the firmly bolted wing of the door, so that only half his body was visible, as well as his head, tilted sideways, with which he peeped over at the others. Meanwhile it had become much brighter. Standing out clearly from the other side of the street was a section of the endless grey-black house situated opposite—it was a hospital—with its severe regular windows breaking up the facade. The rain was still coming down, but only in large individual drops visibly and firmly thrown down one by one onto the ground. Countless breakfast dishes were standing piled around on the table, because for his father breakfast was the most important meal time in the day, which he prolonged for hours by reading various newspapers. Directly across on the opposite wall hung a photograph of Gregor from the time of his military service; it was a picture of him as a lieutenant, as he, smiling and worry free, with his hand on his sword, demanded respect for his bearing and uniform. The door to the hall was ajar, and since the door to the apartment was also open, one could see out into the landing of the apartment and the start of the staircase going down.

"Now," said Gregor, well aware that he was the only one who had kept his composure. "I'll get dressed right away, pack up the collection of samples, and set off. You'll allow me to set out on my way, will you not? You see, Mr. Manager, I am not pig-headed, and I am happy to work. Travelling is exhausting, but I couldn't live without it. Where are you going, Mr. Manager? To the office? Really? Will you report everything truthfully? A person can be incapable of work momentarily, but that's precisely the best time to remember the earlier achievements and to consider that later, after the obstacles have been shoved aside, the person will certainly work all the more diligently and intensely. I am really so indebted to Mr. Chief—you know that perfectly well. On the other hand, I am concerned about my parents and my sister. I'm in a fix, but I'll work myself out of it again. Don't make things more difficult for me than they already are. Speak up on my behalf in the office! People don't like travelling salesmen. I know that. People think they earn pots of money and thus lead a fine life. People don't even have any special reason to think through this judgment more clearly. But you, Mr. Manager, you have a better perspective on what's involved than other people, even, I tell you in total confidence, a better perspective than Mr. Chief himself, who in his capacity as the employer may easily let his judgment make mistakes at the expense of an employee. You also know well enough that the travelling salesman who is outside the office almost the entire year can become so easily a victim of gossip, coincidences, and groundless complaints, against which it's totally impossible for him to defend himself, since for the most part he doesn't hear about them at all and only then when he's exhausted after finishing a trip and at home gets to feel in his own body the nasty consequences, which can't be thoroughly explored back to their origins. Mr. Manager, don't leave without speaking a word indicating to me that you'll at least concede that I'm a little in the right!"

But at Gregor's first words the manager had already turned away, and now he looked back with pursed lips at Gregor over his twitching shoulders. During Gregor's speech he was not still for a moment but kept moving away towards the door, without taking his eyes off Gregor, but really gradually, as if there was a secret ban on leaving the room. He was already in the hall, and, given the sudden movement with which he finally pulled his foot out of the living room, one could have believed that he had just burned the sole of his foot. In the hall, however, he stretched his right hand out away from his body towards the staircase, as if some truly supernatural relief was waiting for him there.

Gregor realized that he must not under any circumstances allow the manager to go away in this frame of mind, especially if his position in the firm was not to be placed in the greatest danger. His parents did not understand all this very well. Over the long years, they had developed the conviction that Gregor was set up for life in this firm and, in addition, they had so much to do nowadays with their present troubles that all foresight was foreign to them. But Gregor had this foresight. The manager must be held back, calmed down, convinced, and finally won over. The future of Gregor and his family really depended on it! If only the sister had been there! She was clever. She had already cried while Gregor was still lying quietly on his back. And the manager, this friend of the ladies, would certainly let himself be guided by her. She would have closed the door to the apartment and talked him out of his fright in the hall. But the sister was not even there. Gregor must deal with it himself. And without thinking that as yet he did not know anything about his present ability to move and without thinking that his speech possibly—indeed probably—had once again not been understood, he left the wing of the door, pushed himself through the opening, and wanted to go over to the manager, who was already holding tight with both hands gripping the handrail on the landing in a ridiculous way. But as Gregor looked for something to steady himself, with a small scream he immediately fell down onto his numerous little legs. Scarcely had this happened, when he felt for the first time that morning a general physical well being. The small limbs had firm floor under them; they obeyed perfectly, as he noticed to his joy, and even strove to carry him forward in the direction he wanted. Right away he believed that the final amelioration of all his suffering was immediately at hand. But at the very moment when he lay on the floor rocking in a restrained manner quite close and directly across from his mother, who had apparently totally sunk into herself, she suddenly sprang right up with her arms spread far apart and her fingers extended and cried out, "Help, for God's sake, help!" She held her head bowed down, as if she wanted to view Gregor better, but ran senselessly back, contradicting that gesture, forgetting that behind her stood the table with all the dishes on it. When she reached the table, she sat down heavily on it, as if absentmindedly, and did not appear to notice at all that next to her coffee was pouring out onto the carpet in a full stream from the large, overturned container.

"Mother, mother," said Gregor quietly and looked over towards her. The manager had momentarily vanished completely from his mind. On the other hand, when he saw the flowing coffee Gregor could not stop himself snapping his jaws in the air a few times. At that his mother screamed all over again, hurried from the table, and collapsed into the arms of his father, who was rushing towards her. But Gregor had no time right now for his parents—the manager was already on the staircase. With his chin on the bannister, the manager looked back for the last time. Gregor took an initial movement to catch up to him if possible. But the manager must have suspected something, because he made a leap down over a few stairs and disappeared, still shouting "Huh!" The sound echoed throughout the entire stairwell.

But now unfortunately this flight of the manager seemed to bewilder his father completely. Earlier he had been relatively calm. For instead of running after the manager himself or at least not hindering Gregor from his pursuit, with his right hand he grabbed hold of the manager's cane, which he had left behind on a chair with his hat and overcoat. With his left hand, his father grabbed a large newspaper from the table and, stamping his feet on the floor, he set out to drive Gregor back into his room by waving the cane and the newspaper. No request of Gregor's was of any use; no request would even be understood. No matter how willing he was to turn his head respectfully, his father just stomped all the harder with his feet. Across the room from him his mother had pulled open a window, in spite of the cool weather, and leaning out with her hands on her cheeks, she pushed her face far outside the window. Between the lane and the stairwell a strong draught came up, the curtains on the window flew around, the newspapers on the table rustled, and individual sheets fluttered down over the floor. The father relentlessly pushed his way forward, hissing like a wild man. Now, Gregor still had no practice at all in going backwards—it was really very slow going. If Gregor only had been allowed to turn himself around, he would have been in his room right away, but he was afraid to make his father impatient by the time-consuming process of turning around, and each moment he faced the threat of a mortal blow on his back or his head from the cane in his father's hand. Finally Gregor had no other option, for he noticed with horror that he did not understand yet how to maintain his direction going backwards. And so he began, amid constantly anxious sideways glances in his father's direction, to turn himself around as quickly as possible, although in truth this was only done very slowly. Perhaps his father noticed his good intentions, for he did not disrupt Gregor in this motion, but with the tip of the cane from a distance he even directed Gregor's rotating movement now and then. If only his father had not hissed so unbearably! Because of that Gregor totally lost his head. He was already almost totally turned around, when, always with this hissing in his ear, he just made a mistake and turned himself back a little. But when he finally was successful in getting his head in front of the door opening, it became clear that his body was too wide to go through any further. Naturally his father, in his present mental state, had no idea of, say, opening the other wing of the door a bit to create a suitable passage for Gregor to get through. His single fixed thought was that Gregor must get into his room as quickly as possible. He would never have allowed the elaborate preparations that Gregor required to orient himself and thus perhaps in this way to get through the door. Perhaps with his excessive noise he was now driving Gregor forwards as if there were no obstacle. Behind Gregor the sound at this point was no longer like the voice of only a single father. Now it was really no longer a joke, and Gregor forced himself, come what might, into the door. One side of his body was lifted up. He lay at an angle in the door opening. His one flank was really sore from the scraping.

On the white door ugly blotches were left. Soon he was stuck fast and would not have been able to move any more on his own. The tiny legs on one side hung twitching in the air above, and the ones on the other side were pushed painfully into the floor. Then his father gave him one really strong liberating push from behind, and he scurried, bleeding severely, far into the interior of his room. The door was slammed shut with the cane, and then finally it was quiet.

II

Gregor first woke up from his heavy swoon-like sleep in the evening twilight. He would certainly have woken up soon afterwards even without any disturbance, for he felt himself sufficiently rested and wide awake, although it appeared to him as if a hurried step and a cautious closing of the door to the hall had roused him. Light from the electric streetlamps lay pale here and there on the ceiling of his room and on the higher parts of the furniture, but underneath around Gregor it was dark. He pushed himself slowly toward the door, still groping awkwardly with his feelers, which he now learned to value for the first time, to check what was happening there. His left side seemed one single long unpleasantly stretched scar, and he really had to hobble on his two rows of legs. In addition, one small leg had been seriously wounded in the course of the morning incident—it was almost a miracle that only one had been hurt—and dragged lifelessly behind.

By the door he first noticed what had really lured him there: it was the smell of something to eat. For a bowl stood there, filled with sweetened milk, in which swam tiny pieces of white bread. He almost laughed with joy, for he had an even greater hunger than in the morning, and he immediately dipped his head almost up to and over his eyes down into the milk. But he soon drew it back again in disappointment, not just because it was difficult for him to eat on account of his delicate left side—he could eat only if his entire panting body worked in a coordinated way—but also because the milk, which otherwise was his favourite drink and which his sister had certainly placed there for that reason, did not appeal to him at all. He turned away from the bowl almost with aversion and crept back into the middle of the room.

In the living room, as Gregor saw through the crack in the door, the gas was lit, but where, on other occasions at this time of day, his father was accustomed to read the afternoon newspaper in a loud voice to his mother and sometimes also to his sister, at the moment no sound was audible. Now, perhaps this reading aloud, about which his sister had always spoken and written to him, had recently fallen out of their general routine. But it was so still all around, in spite of the fact that the apartment was certainly not empty. "What a quiet life the family leads," said Gregor to himself, and, as he stared fixedly out in front of him into the darkness, he felt a great pride that he had been able to provide such a life for his parents and his sister in such a beautiful apartment. But how would things go if now all tranquillity, all prosperity, all contentment should come to a horrible end? In order not to lose himself in such thoughts, Gregor preferred to set himself moving, so he crawled up and down in his room.

Once during the long evening one side door and then the other door were opened just a tiny crack and quickly closed again. Someone presumably needed to come in but had then thought better of it. Gregor immediately took up a position by the living room door, determined to bring in the hesitant visitor somehow or other or at least to find out who it might be. But now the door was not opened any more, and Gregor waited in vain. Earlier, when the door had been barred, they had all wanted to come in to him; now, when he had opened one door and when the others had obviously been opened during the day, no one came any more, and now the keys were stuck in the locks on the outside.

The light in the living room was turned off only late at night, and it was now easy to establish that his parents and his sister had stayed awake all this time, for one could hear them clearly as all three moved away on tiptoe. Now it was certain that no one would come in to Gregor any more until the morning. Thus, he had a long time to think undisturbed about how he should reorganize his life from scratch. But the high, open room, in which he was compelled to lie flat on the floor, made him anxious, without his being able to figure out the reason, for he had lived in the room for five years. With a half-unconscious turn and not without a little shame he scurried under the couch, where, in spite of the fact that his back was a little cramped and he could no longer lift up his head, he felt very comfortable right away and was sorry only that his body was too wide to fit completely under the couch.

There he remained the entire night, which he spent partly in a state of semi-sleep, out of which his hunger constantly woke him with a start, but partly in a state of worry and murky hopes, which all led to the conclusion that for the time being he would have to keep calm and with patience and the greatest consideration for his family tolerate the troubles which in his present condition he was now forced to cause them.

Already early in the morning—it was still almost night—Gregor had an opportunity to test the power of the decisions he had just made, for his sister, almost fully dressed, opened the door from the hall into his room and looked eagerly inside. She did not find him immediately, but when she noticed him under the couch— God, he had to be somewhere or other, for he could hardly fly away—she got such a shock that, without being able to control herself, she slammed the door shut once again from the outside. However, as if she was sorry for her behaviour, she immediately opened the door again and walked in on her tiptoes, as if she was in the presence of a serious invalid or a total stranger. Gregor had pushed his head forward just to the edge of the couch and was observing her. Would she really notice that he had left the milk standing, not indeed from any lack of hunger, and would she bring in something else to eat more suitable for him? If she did not do it on her own, he would sooner starve to death than call her attention to the fact, although he had a really powerful urge to move beyond the couch, throw himself at his sister's feet, and beg her for something or other good to eat. But his sister noticed right away with astonishment that the bowl was still full, with only a little milk spilled around it. She picked it up immediately, although not with her bare hands but with a rag, and took it out of the room. Gregor was extremely curious what she would bring as a substitute, and he pictured to himself very different ideas about it. But he never could have guessed what his sister, out of the goodness of her heart, in fact, did. To test his taste, she brought him an entire selection, all spread out on an old newspaper. There were old half-rotten vegetables, bones from the evening meal, covered with a white sauce which had almost solidified, some raisins and almonds, cheese which Gregor had declared inedible two days earlier, a slice of dry bread, a slice with butter, and a slice of salted bread smeared with butter. In addition to all this, she put down the bowl—probably designated once and for all as Gregor's—into which she had poured some water. And out of her delicacy of feeling, since she knew that Gregor would not eat in front of her, she went away very quickly and even turned the key in the lock, so that Gregor could now know that he might make himself as comfortable as he wished. Gregor's small limbs buzzed now that the time for eating had come. His wounds must, in any case, have already healed completely. He felt no handicap on that score. He was astonished at that and thought about how more than a month ago he had cut his finger very slightly with a knife and how this wound had hurt enough even the day before yesterday. "Am I now going to be less sensitive?" he thought, already sucking greedily on the cheese, which had strongly attracted him right away, more than all the other foods. Quickly and with his eyes watering with satisfaction, he ate one after the other the cheese, the vegetables, and the sauce. The fresh food, by contrast, did not taste good to him. He could not even bear the smell and carried the things he wanted to eat a little distance away. By the time his sister slowly turned the key as a sign that he should withdraw, he was long finished with everything and now lay lazily in the same spot. The noise immediately startled him, in spite of the fact that he was already almost asleep, and he scurried back again under the couch. But it cost him great self-control to remain under the couch, even for the short time his sister was in the room, because his body had filled out somewhat on account of the rich meal and in the narrow space there he could scarcely breathe.

In the midst of minor attacks of asphyxiation, he looked at her with somewhat protruding eyes, as his unsuspecting sister swept up with a broom, not just the remnants, but even the foods which Gregor had not touched at all, as if these were also now useless, and as she dumped everything quickly into a bucket, which she closed with a wooden lid, and then carried all of it out of the room. She had hardly turned around before Gregor had already dragged himself out from under the couch, stretched out, and let his body expand.

In this way Gregor now got his food every day, once in the morning, when his parents and the servant girl were still asleep, and a second time after the common noon meal, for his parents were asleep then for a little while, and the servant girl was sent off by his sister on some errand or other. They certainly would not have wanted Gregor to starve to death, but perhaps they could not have endured finding out what he ate other than by hearsay. Perhaps his sister also wanted to spare them what was possibly only a small grief, for they were really suffering quite enough already.

What sorts of excuses people had used on that first morning to get the doctor and the locksmith out of the house again Gregor was completely unable to ascertain. Since they could not understand him, no one, not even his sister, thought that he might be able to understand others, and thus, when his sister was in his room, he had to be content with listening now and then to her sighs and invocations to the saints. Only later, when she had grown somewhat accustomed to everything—naturally there could never be any talk of her growing completely accustomed to it—Gregor sometimes caught a comment which was intended to be friendly or could be interpreted as such. "Well, today it tasted good to him," she said, if Gregor had really cleaned up what he had to eat; whereas, in the reverse situation, which gradually repeated itself more and more frequently, she used to say almost sadly, "Now everything has been left again."

But while Gregor could get no new information directly, he did hear a good deal from the room next door, and as soon as he heard voices, he scurried right away to the appropriate door and pressed his entire body against it. In the early days especially, there was no conversation which was not concerned with him in some way or other, even if only in secret. For two days at all meal times discussions of that subject could be heard on how people should now behave; but they also talked about the same subject in the times between meals, for there were always at least two family members at home, since no one really wanted to remain in the house alone and people could not under any circumstances leave the apartment completely empty. In addition, on the very first day the servant girl—it was not completely clear what and how much she knew about what had happened—on her knees had begged his mother to let her go immediately, and when she said good bye about fifteen minutes later, she thanked them for the dismissal with tears in her eyes, as if she was receiving the greatest favour which people had shown her there, and, without anyone demanding it from her, she swore a fearful oath not to reveal anything to anyone, not even the slightest detail.

Now his sister had to team up with his mother to do the cooking, although that did not create much trouble because people were eating almost nothing. Again and again Gregor listened as one of them vainly invited another one to eat and received no answer other than "Thank you. I've had enough" or something like that. And perhaps they had stopped having anything to drink, too. His sister often asked his father whether he wanted to have a beer and gladly offered to fetch it herself, and when his father was silent, she said, in order to remove any reservations he might have, that she could send the caretaker's wife to get it. But then his father finally said a resounding "No," and nothing more would be spoken about it.

Already during the first day his father laid out all the financial circumstances and prospects to his mother and to his sister as well. From time to time he stood up from the table and pulled out of the small lockbox salvaged from his business, which had collapsed five years previously, some document or other or some notebook. The sound was audible as he opened up the complicated lock and, after removing what he was looking for, locked it up again. These explanations by his father were, in part, the first enjoyable thing that Gregor had the chance to listen to since his imprisonment. He had thought that nothing at all was left over for his father from that business; at least his father had told him nothing to contradict that view, and Gregor in any case had not asked him about it. At the time Gregor's only concern had been to use everything he had in order to allow his family to forget as quickly as possible the business misfortune which had brought them all into a state of complete hopelessness. And so at that point he had started to work with a special intensity and from a minor assistant had become, almost overnight, a travelling salesman, who naturally had entirely different possibilities for earning money and whose successes at work were converted immediately into the form of cash commissions, which could be set out on the table at home for his astonished and delighted family. Those had been beautiful days, and they had never come back afterwards, at least not with the same splendour, in spite of the fact that Gregor later earned so much money that he was in a position to bear the expenses of the entire family, costs which he, in fact, did bear. They had become quite accustomed to it, both the family and Gregor as well. They took the money with thanks, and he happily surrendered it, but a special warmth was no longer present. Only the sister had remained still close to Gregor, and it was his secret plan to send her next year to the Conservatory, regardless of the great expense which that necessarily involved and which would be made up in other ways. In contrast to Gregor, she loved music very much and knew how to play the violin charmingly. Now and then during Gregor's short stays in the city the Conservatory was mentioned in conversations with his sister, but always merely as a beautiful dream, whose realization was unimaginable, and their parents never listened to these innocent expectations with pleasure. But Gregor thought about them with scrupulous consideration and intended to explain the matter in all seriousness on Christmas Eve.

In his present situation, such completely futile ideas went through his head, while he pushed himself right up against the door and listened. Sometimes in his general exhaustion he could not listen any more and let his head bang listlessly against the door, but he immediately pulled himself together once more, for even the small sound which he made by this motion was heard near by and silenced everyone. "There he goes on again," said his father after a while, clearly turning towards the door, and only then would the interrupted conversation gradually be resumed again.

Now, Gregor found out clearly enough—for his father tended to repeat himself from time to time in his explanations, partly because he had not personally concerned himself with these matters for a long time now, and partly because his mother did not understand everything right away the first time—that, in spite all bad luck, an amount of money, although a very small one, was still available from the old times and that the interest, which had not been touched, had in the intervening time allowed it to increase a little. Furthermore, in addition to this, the money which Gregor had brought home every month—he had kept only a few crowns for himself—had not been completely spent and had grown into a small capital amount. Gregor, behind his door, nodded eagerly, rejoicing over this unanticipated foresight and frugality. True, with this excess money, he could really have paid off more of his father's debt to his employer and the day on which he could be rid of this position would have been a lot closer, but now things were doubtless better the way his father had arranged them.

At the moment, however, this money was not nearly sufficient to permit the family to live on the interest payments. Perhaps it would be enough to maintain the family for one or at most two years, that was all. Thus, it only added up to an amount which one should not really draw upon and which must be set aside for an emergency. But they had to earn money to live on. Now, it's true his father was indeed a healthy man, but he was old and had not worked for five years and thus could not be counted on for very much. He had in these five years, the first holidays of his laborious but unsuccessful life, put on a good deal of fat and thus had become really heavy. And should his old mother now perhaps work for money, a woman who suffered from asthma, for whom wandering through the apartment even now was a great strain and who spent every second day on the sofa by the open window having trouble with her breathing? Should his sister earn money, a girl who was still a seventeen-year-old child and whose earlier life style had been so very delightful that it had consisted of dressing herself nicely, sleeping in late, helping around the house, taking part in a few modest enjoyments and, above all, playing the violin? When it came to talking about this need to earn money, at first Gregor went away from the door and threw himself on the cool leather sofa beside the door, for he was quite hot from shame and sorrow.

Often he lay there all night long, not sleeping at all, just scratching on the leather for hours at a time. Or he undertook the very difficult task of pushing a chair over to the window. Then he crept up on the window sill and, braced on the chair, leaned against the window to look out, obviously with some memory or other of the liberating sense which looking out the window used to bring him in earlier times. For, in fact, from day to day he perceived things with less and less clarity, even those only a short distance away. The hospital across the street, the all-too-frequent sight of which he had previously cursed, was not visible at all any more, and if he had not been very well aware that he lived in the quiet but completely urban Charlotte Street, he could have believed that from his window he was peering out at a featureless wasteland, in which the grey heaven and the grey earth had merged and were indistinguishable. His observant sister only had to notice a couple of times that the chair stood by the window; then, after cleaning up the room, each time, she pushed the chair back right against the window again and from now on she even left the inner casements open.

If Gregor had only been able to speak to his sister and thank her for everything that she had to do for him, he would have tolerated her service more easily. As it was, he suffered under it. The sister admittedly sought to cover up the awkwardness of everything as much as possible, and, as time went by, she naturally became more successful at it. But with the passing of time Gregor also came to understand everything much more clearly. Even her entrance was terrible for him. As soon as she came in, she ran straight to the window, without taking the time to shut the door, in spite of the fact that she was otherwise very considerate in sparing anyone the sight of Gregor's room, and yanked the window open with eager hands, as if she was almost suffocating, and remained for a while by the window breathing deeply, even when it was still so cold. With this running and noise she frightened Gregor twice every day. The entire time he trembled under the couch, and yet he knew very well that she would certainly have spared him gladly if it had only been possible to remain with the window closed in a room where Gregor lived.

On one occasion—about one month had already gone by since Gregor's transformation, and there was now no particular reason any more for his sister to be startled at Gregor's appearance—she arrived a little earlier than usual and came upon Gregor as he was still looking out the window, immobile and well positioned to frighten someone. It would not have come as a surprise to Gregor if she had not come in, since his position was preventing her from opening the window immediately. But not only did she not step inside; she even retreated and shut the door. A stranger really could have concluded from this that Gregor had been lying in wait for her and wanted to bite her. Of course, Gregor immediately concealed himself under the couch, but he had to wait until noon before his sister returned, and she seemed much less calm than usual. From this he realized that his appearance was still intolerable to her and must remain intolerable to her in future, and that she really had to exert a lot of self-control not to run away from a glimpse of only the small part of his body which stuck out from under the couch. In order to spare her even this sight, one day he dragged the sheet on his back and onto the couch—this task took him four hours—and arranged it in such a way that he was now completely concealed and his sister, even if she bent down, could not see him. If this sheet was not necessary as far as she was concerned, then she could remove it, for it was clear enough that Gregor could not derive any pleasure from isolating himself away so completely. But she left the sheet just as it was, and Gregor believed he even caught a look of gratitude when, on one occasion, he carefully lifted up the sheet a little with his head to check, as his sister took stock of the new arrangement.

In the first two weeks his parents could not bring themselves to visit him, and he often heard how they fully acknowledged his sister's present work; whereas, earlier they had often got annoyed at his sister because she had seemed to them a somewhat useless young woman. However, now both his father and his mother frequently waited in front of Gregor's door while his sister cleaned up inside, and as soon as she came out, she had to explain in great detail how things looked in the room, what Gregor had eaten, how he had behaved this time, and whether perhaps a slight improvement was perceptible. In any event, his mother comparatively soon wanted to visit Gregor, but his father and his sister restrained her, at first with reasons which Gregor listened to very attentively and which he completely endorsed. Later, however, they had to hold her back forcefully, and when she then cried "Let me go to Gregor. He's my unfortunate son! Don't you understand that I have to go to him?" Gregor then thought that perhaps it would be a good thing if his mother came in, not every day, of course, but maybe once a week. She understood everything much better than his sister, who, in spite of all her courage, was still merely a child and, in the last analysis, had perhaps undertaken such a difficult task only out of childish recklessness.

Gregor's wish to see his mother was soon realized. While during the day Gregor, out of consideration for his parents, did not want to show himself by the window, he could not crawl around very much on the few square metres of the floor. He found it difficult to bear lying quietly during the night, and soon eating no longer gave him the slightest pleasure. So for diversion he acquired the habit of crawling back and forth across the walls and ceiling. He was especially fond of hanging from the ceiling. The experience was quite different from lying on the floor. It was easier to breathe, a slight vibration went through his body, and in the midst of the almost happy amusement which Gregor found up there, it could happen that, to his own surprise, he let go and hit the floor. However, now he naturally controlled his body quite differently than before, and he did not injure himself in such a great fall. Now, his sister noticed immediately the new amusement which Gregor had found for himself—for as he crept around he left behind here and there traces of his sticky stuff—and so she got the idea of making the area where Gregor could creep around as large as possible and thus of removing the furniture which got in the way, especially the chest of drawers and the writing desk. But she was in no position to do this by herself. She did not dare to ask her father to help, and the servant girl would certainly not have assisted her, for although this girl, about sixteen years old, had courageously remained since the dismissal of the previous cook, she had begged for the privilege of being allowed to stay permanently confined to the kitchen and of having to open the door only in answer to a special summons. Thus, his sister had no other choice but to involve his mother at a time when his father was absent. His mother approached Gregor's room with cries of excited joy, but she fell silent at the door. Of course, his sister first checked whether everything in the room was in order. Only then did she let his mother enter. Gregor had drawn the sheet down with the greatest haste even further and wrinkled it more. The whole thing really looked just like a coverlet thrown carelessly over the couch. On this occasion, Gregor also held back from spying out from under the sheet. He refrained from looking at his mother this time and was merely happy that she had now come. "Come on. You can't see him," said his sister and evidently led his mother by the hand. Now Gregor listened as these two weak women shifted the still heavy old chest of drawers from its position and as his sister constantly took on herself the greatest part of the work, without listening to the warnings of his mother, who was afraid that she would strain herself. The work lasted a very long time. After about a quarter of an hour had already gone by, his mother said it would be better if they left the chest of drawers where it was, because, in the first place, it was too heavy: they would not be finished before his father's arrival, and leaving the chest of drawers in the middle of the room would block all Gregor's pathways, but, in the second place, they could not be at all certain that Gregor would be pleased with the removal of the furniture. To her the reverse seemed to be true; the sight of the empty walls pierced her right to the heart, and why should Gregor not feel the same, since he had been accustomed to the room furnishings for a long time and would therefore feel himself abandoned in an empty room. "And is it not the case," his mother concluded very quietly, almost whispering, as if she wished to prevent Gregor, whose exact location she really did not know, from hearing even the sound of her voice—for she was convinced that he did not understand her words—"and isn't it a fact that by removing the furniture we're showing that we're giving up all hope of an improvement and are leaving him to his own resources without any consideration? I think it would be best if we tried to keep the room exactly in the condition it was in before, so that, when Gregor returns to us, he finds everything unchanged and can forget the intervening time all the more easily."

As he heard his mother's words Gregor realized that the lack of all immediate human contact, together with the monotonous life surrounded by the family over the course of these two months, must have confused his understanding, because otherwise he could not explain to himself how he, in all seriousness, could have been so keen to have his room emptied. Was he really eager to let the warm room, comfortably furnished with pieces he had inherited, be turned into a cavern in which he would, of course, then be able to crawl about in all directions without disturbance, but at the same time with a quick and complete forgetting of his human past as well? Was he then at this point already on the verge of forgetting and was it only the voice of his mother, which he had not heard for a long time, that had aroused him? Nothing was to be removed—everything must remain. In his condition he could not function without the beneficial influences of his furniture. And if the furniture prevented him from carrying out his senseless crawling about all over the place, then there was no harm in that, but rather a great benefit.

But his sister unfortunately thought otherwise. She had grown accustomed, certainly not without justification, so far as the discussion of matters concerning Gregor was concerned, to act as a special expert with respect to their parents, and so now the mother's advice was for his sister sufficient reason to insist on the removal, not only of the chest of drawers and the writing desk, which were the only items she had thought about at first, but also of all the furniture, with the exception of the indispensable couch. Of course, it was not only childish defiance and her recent very unexpected and hard won self-confidence which led her to this demand. She had also actually observed that Gregor needed a great deal of room to creep about; the furniture, on the other hand, as far as one could see, was not the slightest use. But perhaps the enthusiastic sensibility of young women of her age also played a role. This feeling sought release at every opportunity, and with it Grete now felt tempted to want to make Gregor's situation even more terrifying, so that then she would be able to do even more for him than she had up to now. For surely no one except Grete would ever trust themselves to enter a room in which Gregor ruled the empty walls all by himself.

And so she did not let herself be dissuaded from her decision by her mother, who in this room seemed uncertain of herself in her sheer agitation and soon kept quiet, helping his sister with all her energy to get the chest of drawers out of the room. Now, Gregor could still do without the chest of drawers if need be, but the writing desk really had to stay. And scarcely had the women left the room with the chest of drawers, groaning as they pushed it, when Gregor stuck his head out from under the sofa to see how he could intervene, cautiously and with as much consideration as possible. But unfortunately it was his mother who came back into the room first, while Grete had her arms wrapped around the chest of drawers in the next room and was rocking it back and forth by herself, of course without moving it from its position. But his mother was not used to the sight of Gregor; he could have made her ill, and so, frightened, Gregor scurried backwards right to the other end of the sofa. However, he could no longer prevent the sheet from moving forward a little. That was enough to catch his mother's attention. She came to a halt, stood still for a moment, and then went back to Grete.

Although Gregor kept repeating to himself over and over that really nothing unusual was going on, that only a few pieces of furniture were being rearranged, he soon had to admit to himself that the movements of the women to and fro, their quiet conversations, and the scraping of the furniture on the floor affected him like a great commotion stirred up on all sides, and, so firmly was he pulling in his head and legs and pressing his body into the floor, he had to tell himself unequivocally that he would not be able to endure all this much longer. They were cleaning out his room, taking away from him everything he cherished; they had already dragged out the chest of drawers in which the fret saw and other tools were kept, and they were now loosening the writing desk which was fixed tight to the floor, the desk on which he, as a business student, a school student, indeed even as an elementary school student, had written out his assignments. At that moment he really did not have any more time to check the good intentions of the two women, whose existence he had in any case almost forgotten, because in their exhaustion they were working really silently, and the heavy stumbling of their feet was the only sound to be heard.

And so he scuttled out—the women were just propping themselves up on the writing desk in the next room in order to take a short breather. He changed the direction of his path four times. He really did not know what he should rescue first. Then he saw hanging conspicuously on the wall, which was otherwise already empty, the picture of the woman dressed in nothing but fur. He quickly scurried up over it and pressed himself against the glass which held it in place and which made his hot abdomen feel good. At least this picture, which Gregor at the moment completely concealed, surely no one would now take away. He twisted his head towards the door of the living room to observe the women as they came back in.

They had not allowed themselves very much rest and were coming back right away. Grete had placed her arm around her mother and held her tightly. "So what shall we take now?" said Grete and looked around her. Then her glance met Gregor's from the wall. She kept her composure only because her mother was there. She bent her face towards her mother in order to prevent her from looking around, and said, although in a trembling voice and too quickly, "Come, wouldn't it be better to go back to the living room for just another moment?" Grete's purpose was clear to Gregor: she wanted to bring his mother to a safe place and then chase him down from the wall. Well, let her just try! He squatted on his picture and did not hand it over. He would sooner spring into Grete's face.

But Grete's words had immediately made the mother very uneasy. She walked to the side, caught sight of the enormous brown splotch on the flowered wallpaper, and, before she became truly aware that what she was looking at was Gregor, screamed out in a high-pitched raw voice "Oh God, oh God" and fell with outstretched arms, as if she was surrendering everything, down onto the couch and lay there motionless. "Gregor, you. . ." cried out his sister with a raised fist and an urgent glare. Since his transformation these were the first words which she had directed right at him. She ran into the room next door to bring some spirits or other with which she could revive her mother from her fainting spell. Gregor wanted to help as well—there was time enough to save the picture—but he was stuck fast on the glass and had to tear himself loose forcibly. Then he also scurried into the next room, as if he could give his sister some advice, as in earlier times, but then he had to stand there idly behind her, while she rummaged about among various small bottles. Still, she was frightened when she turned around. A bottle fell onto the floor and shattered. A splinter of glass wounded Gregor in the face, and some corrosive medicine or other dripped over him. Now, without lingering any longer, Grete took as many small bottles as she could hold and ran with them in to her mother. She slammed the door shut with her foot. Gregor was now shut off from his mother, who was perhaps near death, thanks to him. He could not open the door; he did not want to chase away his sister, who had to remain with her mother. At this point he had nothing to do but wait, and, overwhelmed with self-reproach and worry, he began to creep and crawl over everything: walls, furniture, and ceiling. Finally, in his despair, as the entire room started to spin around him, he fell onto the middle of the large table.

A short time elapsed. Gregor lay there limply. All around was still. Perhaps that was a good sign. Then there was ring at the door. The servant girl was naturally shut up in her kitchen, and therefore Grete had to go to open the door. The father had arrived. "What's happened?" were his first words. Grete's appearance had told him everything. Grete replied with a dull voice; evidently she was pressing her face against her father's chest: "Mother fainted, but she's getting better now. Gregor has broken loose." "Yes, I have expected that," said his father, "I always warned you of that, but you women don't want to listen." It was clear to Gregor that his father had badly misunderstood Grete's all-too-brief message and was assuming that Gregor had committed some violent crime or other. Thus, Gregor now had to find his father to calm him down, for he had neither the time nor the ability to explain things to him. And so he rushed away to the door of his room and pushed himself against it, so that his father could see right away as he entered from the hall that Gregor fully intended to return at once to his room, that it was not necessary to drive him back, but that one only needed to open the door, and he would disappear immediately.

But his father was not in the mood to observe such niceties. "Ah!" he yelled as soon as he entered, with a tone as if he were at once angry and pleased. Gregor pulled his head back from the door and raised it in the direction of his father. He had not really pictured his father as he now stood there. Of course, what with his new style of creeping all around, he had in the past while neglected to pay attention to what was going on in the rest of the apartment, as he had done before, and really should have grasped the fact that he would encounter different conditions. And yet, and yet, was that still his father? Was that the same man who had lain exhausted and buried in bed in earlier days when Gregor was setting out on a business trip, who had received him on the evenings of his return in a sleeping gown and arm chair, totally incapable of standing up, who had only lifted his arm as a sign of happiness, and who in their rare strolls together a few Sundays a year and on the most important holidays made his way slowly forwards between Gregor and his mother—who themselves moved slowly—always a bit more slowly than them, bundled up in his old coat, working hard to move forwards and always setting down his walking stick carefully, and who, when he had wanted to say something, almost always stood still and gathered his entourage around him? But now he was standing up really straight, dressed in a tight-fitting blue uniform with gold buttons, like the ones servants wear in a banking company. Above the high stiff collar of his jacket his firm double chin stuck out prominently, beneath his bushy eyebrows the glance of his black eyes was fresh and alert, and his usually dishevelled white hair was combed down into a shining and carefully exact parting. He threw his cap, on which a gold monogram, probably the symbol of a bank, was affixed, in an arc across the entire room onto the sofa and, thrusting back the edges of the long coat of his uniform, with his hands in his trouser pockets and a grim face, moved right up to Gregor. He really did not know what he had in mind, but he raised his foot uncommonly high anyway, and Gregor was astonished at the gigantic size of the sole of his boot. However, he did not linger on that point, for he had known even from the first day of his new life that, as far as he was concerned, his father considered the only appropriate response to be the greatest force. And so he scurried away from his father, stopped when his father remained standing, and scampered forward again when his father merely stirred. In this way they made their way around the room repeatedly, without anything decisive taking place. In fact, because of the slow pace, it did not look like a chase. So Gregor remained on the floor for the time being, especially since he was afraid that his father could interpret a flight up onto the wall or the ceiling as an act of real malice. At any event, Gregor had to tell himself that he could not keep up this running around for a long time, because whenever his father took a single step, he had to go through a large number of movements. Already he was starting to feel a shortage of breath, just as in his earlier days when his lungs had been quite unreliable. As he now staggered around in this way in order to gather all his energies for running, hardly keeping his eyes open and feeling so listless that he had no notion at all of any escape other than by running and had almost already forgotten that the walls were available to him, although here they were obstructed by carefully carved furniture full of sharp points and spikes, at that moment something or other thrown casually flew close by and rolled in front of him. It was an apple. Immediately a second one flew after it. Gregor stood still in fright. Further running away was useless, for his father had decided to bombard him. From the fruit bowl on the sideboard his father had filled his pockets, and now, without for the moment taking accurate aim, he was throwing apple after apple. These small red apples rolled around on the floor, as if electrified, and collided with each other. A weakly thrown apple grazed Gregor's back but skidded off harmlessly. However, another thrown immediately after that one drove into Gregor's back really hard. Gregor wanted to drag himself off, as if he could make the unexpected and incredible pain go away if he changed his position. But he felt as if he was nailed in place and lay stretched out completely confused in all his senses. Only with his final glance did he notice how the door of his room was pulled open and how, right in front of his screaming sister, his mother ran out in her underbodice, for his sister had loosened her clothing in order to give her some freedom to breathe in her fainting spell, and how his mother then ran up to his father—on the way her loosened petticoats slipped toward the floor one after the other—and how, tripping over them, she hurled herself onto his father and, throwing her arms around him, in complete union with him—but at this moment Gregor's powers of sight gave way—as her hands reached around his father's neck, and she begged him to spare Gregor's life.

III

Gregor's serious wound, from which he suffered for over a month —since no one ventured to remove the apple, it remained in his flesh as a visible reminder—seemed by itself to have reminded the father that, in spite of Gregor's present unhappy and hateful appearance, he was a member of the family and should not be treated as an enemy, but that it was, on the contrary, a requirement of family duty to suppress one's aversion and to endure— nothing else, just endure.

And if through his wound Gregor had now also apparently lost for good his ability to move and for the time being needed many, many minutes to crawl across his room, like an aged invalid—so far as creeping up high was concerned, that was unimaginable— nevertheless, for this worsening of his condition, in his view he did get completely satisfactory compensation, because every day towards evening the door to the living room, which he was in the habit of keeping a sharp eye on even one or two hours before- hand, was opened, so that he, lying down in the darkness of his room, invisible from the living room, could see the entire family at the illuminated table and listen to their conversation, to a certain extent with their common permission, a situation quite different from what had happened before.

Of course, it was no longer the animated social interaction of former times, which in small hotel rooms Gregor had always thought about with a certain longing, when, tired out, he had had to throw himself into the damp bedclothes. For the most part what went on now was only very quiet. After the evening meal, the father soon fell asleep in his arm chair. The mother and sister warned each other to be quiet. Bent far over the light, the mother sewed fine undergarments for a fashion shop. The sister, who had taken on a job as a salesgirl, in the evening studied stenography and French, so as perhaps to obtain a better position later on. Sometimes the father woke up and, as if he was quite ignorant that he had been asleep, said to the mother "How long you have been sewing again today!" and went right back to sleep, while the mother and the sister smiled tiredly to each other.

With a sort of stubbornness the father refused to take off his servant's uniform even at home, and while his sleeping gown hung unused on the coat hook, the father dozed completely dressed in his place, as if he was always ready for his responsibility and even here was waiting for the voice of his superior. As a result, in spite of all the care from the mother and sister, his uniform, which even at the start was not new, grew dirty, and Gregor looked, often for the entire evening, at this clothing, with stains all over it and with its gold buttons always polished, in which the old man, although very uncomfortable, nonetheless was sleeping peacefully.

As soon as the clock struck ten, the mother tried gently encouraging the father to wake up and then persuading him to go to bed, on the ground that he could not get a proper sleep here and that the father, who had to report for service at six o'clock, really needed a good sleep. But in his stubbornness, which had gripped him since he had become a servant, he always insisted on staying even longer by the table, although he regularly fell asleep and then could be prevailed upon only with the greatest difficulty to trade his chair for the bed. No matter how much the mother and sister might at that point work on him with small admonitions, for a quarter of an hour he would remain shaking his head slowly, his eyes closed, without standing up. The mother would pull him by the sleeve and speak flattering words into his ear; the sister would leave her work to help her mother, but that would not have the desired effect on the father. He would merely settle himself even more deeply into his arm chair. Only when the two women grabbed him under the armpits would he throw his eyes open, look back and forth at the mother and sister, and habitually say "This is a life. This is the peace and quiet of my old age." And propped up by both women, he would heave himself up elaborately, as if for him it was the greatest trouble, allow himself to be led to the door by the women, wave them away there, and proceed on his own from that point, while the mother quickly threw down her sewing implements and the sister her pen in order to run after the father and help him some more.

In this overworked and exhausted family who had time to worry any longer about Gregor more than was absolutely necessary? The household was constantly getting smaller. The servant girl was now let go. A huge bony cleaning woman with white hair flying all over her head came in the morning and evening to do the heaviest work. The mother took care of everything else, in addition to her considerable sewing work. It even happened that various pieces of family jewellery, which previously the mother and sister had been overjoyed to wear on social and festive occasions, were sold, as Gregor found out in the evening from the general discussion of the prices they had fetched. But the greatest complaint was always that they could not leave this apartment, which was much too big for their present means, since it was impossible to imagine how Gregor might be moved. But Gregor fully recognized that it was not just consideration for him which was preventing a move, for he could have been transported easily in a suitable box with a few air holes. The main thing holding the family back from a change in living quarters was far more their complete hopelessness and the idea that they had been struck by a misfortune like no one else in their entire circle of relatives and acquaintances. What the world demands of poor people they now carried out to an extreme degree. The father bought breakfast to the petty officials at the bank, the mother sacrificed herself for the undergarments of strangers, the sister behind her desk was at the beck and call of customers, but the family's energies did not extend any further. And the wound in his back began to pain Gregor all over again, when his mother and sister, after they had escorted the father to bed, now came back, let their work lie, moved close together, and sat cheek to cheek and when his mother would now say, pointing to Gregor's room, "Close the door, Grete," and when Gregor was again in the darkness, while close by the women mingled their tears or, quite dry eyed, stared at the table.

Gregor spent his nights and days with hardly any sleep. Sometimes he thought that the next time the door opened he would take over the family arrangements just as he had earlier. In his imagination appeared again, after a long time, his boss and the manager, the chief clerk and the apprentices, the excessively spineless custodian, two or three friends from other businesses, a chambermaid from a hotel in the provinces, a loving, fleeting memory, a female cashier from a hat shop, whom he had seriously but too slowly courted—they all appeared mixed in with strangers or people he had already forgotten, but instead of helping him and his family, they were all unapproachable, and he was happy to see them disappear. But then again he was in no mood to worry about his family. He was filled with sheer anger over the wretched care he was getting, even though he could not imagine anything which he might have an appetite for. Still, he made plans about how he could get into the larder to take there what he at all accounts deserved, even if he was not hungry. Without thinking any more about how they might be able to give Gregor special pleasure, the sister very quickly kicked some food or other, whatever she felt like, into his room in the morning and at noon, before she ran off to her shop. And in the evening, quite indifferent to whether the food had perhaps only been tasted or, what happened most frequently, remained entirely undisturbed, she whisked it out with one sweep of her broom. The task of cleaning his room, which she now always carried out in the evening, could not have been done any more quickly. Streaks of dirt ran along the walls; here and there lay tangles of dust and garbage. At first, when his sister arrived, Gregor positioned himself in a particularly filthy corner in order with this posture to make something of a protest. But he could well have stayed there for weeks without his sister's doing the job any better. In fact, she perceived the dirt as much as he did, but she had decided just to let it stay. In this business, with a touchiness which was quite new to her and which had generally taken over the entire family, she kept watch to see that the cleaning of Gregor's room remained reserved for her. His mother had once undertaken a major clean up of his room, which she had only completed successfully after using a few buckets of water. But the extensive dampness made Gregor sick, and he lay spread out, embittered and immobile, on the couch. However, the mother's punishment did not fail to materialize. For in the evening the sister had hardly observed the change in Gregor's room before she ran into the living room mightily offended and, in spite of her mother's hand lifted high in entreaty, broke out in a fit of crying. Her parents—the father had, of course, woken up with a start in his armchair—at first looked at her astonished and helpless, until they started to get agitated. Turning to his right, the father heaped reproaches on the mother that she had not left the cleaning of Gregor's room to the sister and, turning to his left, he shouted at the sister that she would no longer be allowed to clean Gregor's room ever again, while the mother tried to pull the father, beside himself in his excitement, into the bed room. The sister, shaken by her crying fit, pounded on the table with her tiny fists, and Gregor hissed at all this, angry that no one thought about shutting the door and sparing him the sight of this commotion.

But even when the sister, exhausted from her daily work, had grown tired of caring for Gregor as she had before, even then the mother did not have to come at all in her place. And Gregor did not have to be neglected. For now the cleaning woman was there. This old widow, whose bony frame had enabled her to survive the worst a long life can offer, had no real horror of Gregor. Without being in the least curious, she had once accidentally opened Gregor's door. At the sight of Gregor, who, totally surprised, began to scamper here and there, although no one was chasing him, she remained standing with her hands folded across her stomach staring at him. Since then she did not fail to open the door furtively a little every morning and evening and look in on Gregor. At first, she also called him to her with words which she probably thought were friendly, like "Come here for a bit, old dung beetle!" or "Hey, look at the old dung beetle!" Addressed in such a manner, Gregor made no answer, but remained motionless in his place, as if the door had not been opened at all. If only, instead of allowing this cleaning woman to disturb him uselessly whenever she felt like it, they had given her orders to clean up his room every day! Once in the early morning—a hard downpour, perhaps already a sign of the coming spring, struck the window panes—when the cleaning woman started up once again with her usual conversation, Gregor was so bitter that he turned towards her, as if for an attack, although slowly and weakly. But instead of being afraid of him, the cleaning woman merely lifted up a chair standing close by the door and, as she stood there with her mouth wide open, her intention was clear: she would close her mouth only when the chair in her hand had been thrown down on Gregor's back. "This goes no further, all right?" she asked, as Gregor turned himself around again, and she placed the chair calmly back in the corner.

Gregor ate hardly anything any more. Only when he chanced to move past the food which had been prepared did he, as a game, take a bit into his mouth, hold it there for hours, and generally spit it out again. At first he thought it might be his sadness over the condition of his room which kept him from eating, but he very soon became reconciled to the alterations in his room. People had grown accustomed to discard in there things which they could not put anywhere else, and at this point there were many such items, now that they had rented one room of the apartment to three lodgers. These solemn gentlemen—all three had full beards, as Gregor once found out through a crack in the door—were meticulously intent on tidiness, not only in their own room but, since they had now rented a room here, in the entire household, particularly in the kitchen. They simply did not tolerate any useless or shoddy stuff. Moreover, for the most part they had brought with them their own pieces of furniture. Thus, many items had become superfluous, and these were not really things one could sell or things people wanted to throw out. All these pieces ended up in Gregor's room, even the box of ashes and the garbage pail from the kitchen. The cleaning woman, always in a great hurry, simply flung anything that was for the moment useless into Gregor's room. Fortunately Gregor generally saw only the relevant object and the hand which held it. The cleaning woman perhaps was intending, when time and opportunity allowed, to take the stuff out again or to throw everything out all at once, but in fact the things remained lying there, wherever they had ended up at the first throw, unless Gregor squirmed his way through the accumulation of junk and moved it. At first he was forced to do this because otherwise there was no room for him to creep around, but later he did it with a growing pleasure, although after such movements, tired to death and feeling wretched, he did not budge again for hours.

Because the lodgers sometimes also took their evening meal at home in the common living room, the door to it stayed shut on many evenings. But Gregor had no trouble at all going without the open door. Already on many evenings when it was open he had not availed himself of it, but, without the family noticing, was stretched out in the darkest corner of his room. However, on one occasion the cleaning woman had left the door to the living room slightly ajar, and it remained open even when the lodgers came in as evening fell and the lights were put on. They sat down at the head of the table, where in earlier days the mother, the father, and Gregor had eaten, unfolded their serviettes, and picked up their knives and forks. The mother immediately appeared in the door with a dish of meat and right behind her the sister with a dish piled high with potatoes. The food gave off a lot of steam. The gentlemen lodgers bent over the plates set before them, as if they wanted to check them before eating, and in fact the one who sat in the middle—for the other two he seemed to serve as the authority—cut off a piece of meat still on the dish, obviously to establish whether it was sufficiently tender and whether or not it should be sent back to the kitchen. He was satisfied, and mother and sister, who had looked on in suspense, began to breathe easily and to smile.

The family itself ate in the kitchen. In spite of that, before the father went into the kitchen, he came into the living room and with a single bow, cap in hand, made a tour of the table. The lodgers rose up collectively and murmured something into their beards. Then, when they were alone, they ate almost in complete silence. It seemed odd to Gregor that, out of all the many different sorts of sounds of eating, what was always audible was their chewing teeth, as if by that Gregor should be shown that people needed their teeth to eat and that nothing could be done even with the most handsome toothless jawbone. "I really do have an appetite," Gregor said to himself sorrowfully, "but not for these things. How these lodgers stuff themselves, and I am dying of hunger!"

On this very evening the violin sounded from the kitchen. Gregor did not remember hearing it all through this period. The lodgers had already ended their night meal, the middle one had pulled out a newspaper and had given each of the other two a page, and they were now leaning back, reading and smoking. When the violin started playing, they became attentive, got up, and went on tiptoe to the hall door, at which they remained standing pressed up against one another. They must have been audible from the kitchen, because the father called out, "Perhaps the gentlemen don't like the playing? It can be stopped at once." "On the contrary," stated the lodger in the middle, "might the young woman not come into us and play in the room here, where it is really much more comfortable and cheerful?" "Oh, certainly," cried the father, as if he were the one playing the violin. The men stepped back into the room and waited. Soon the father came with the music stand, the mother with the sheet music, and the sister with the violin. The sister calmly prepared everything for the recital. The parents, who had never previously rented a room and therefore exaggerated their politeness to the lodgers, dared not sit on their own chairs. The father leaned against the door, his right hand stuck between two buttons of his buttoned-up uniform. The mother, however, accepted a chair offered by one of the lodgers. Since she let the chair stay where the gentleman had chanced to put it, she sat to one side in a corner.

The sister began to play. The father and mother, one on each side, followed attentively the movements of her hands. Attracted by the playing, Gregor had ventured to advance a little further forward, and his head was already in the living room. He scarcely wondered about the fact that recently he had had so little consideration for the others. Earlier this consideration had been something he was proud of. And for that very reason he would have had at this moment more reason to hide away, because as a result of the dust which lay all over his room and flew around with the slightest movement, he was totally covered in dirt. On his back and his sides he carted around with him threads, hair, and remnants of food. His indifference to everything was much too great for him to lie on his back and scour himself on the carpet, as he had done earlier several times a day. In spite of this condition he had no timidity about inching forward a bit on the spotless floor of the living room.

In any case, no one paid him any attention. The family was all caught up in the violin playing. The lodgers, by contrast, who for the moment had placed themselves, hands in their trouser pockets, behind the music stand much too close to the sister, so that they could all see the sheet music, something that must certainly have bothered the sister, soon drew back to the window conversing in low voices with bowed heads, where they then remained, anxiously observed by the father. It now seemed really clear that, having assumed they were to hear a beautiful or entertaining violin recital, they were disappointed; they had had enough of the entire performance and were allowing their peace and quiet to be disturbed only out of politeness. In particular, the way in which they all blew the smoke from their cigars out of their noses and mouths up into the air led one to conclude that they were very irritated. And yet his sister was playing so beautifully. Her face was turned to the side, her eyes following the score intently and sadly. Gregor crept forward still a little further, keeping his head close against the floor in order to be able to catch her gaze if possible. Was he an animal that music so captivated him? For him it was as if the way to the unknown nourishment he craved was revealing itself. He was determined to press forward right up to his sister, to tug at her dress, and to indicate to her in this way that she might still come with her violin into his room, because here no one valued the recital as he wanted to value it. He did not wish to let her go from his room any more, at least not so long as he lived. His frightening appearance would for the first time become useful for him. He wanted to be at all the doors of his room simultaneously and snarl back at the attackers. However, his sister should not be compelled but would remain with him voluntarily. She would sit next to him on the sofa, bend down her ear to him, and he would then confide in her that he firmly intended to send her to the Conservatory and that, if his misfortune had not arrived in the interim, he would have declared all this last Christmas—had Christmas really already come and gone?—and would have brooked no argument. After this explanation his sister would break out in tears of emotion, and Gregor would lift himself up to her armpit and kiss her throat, which she, from the time she had been going to work, had left exposed without a band or a collar.

"Mr. Samsa!" called out the middle lodger to the father and, without uttering a further word, pointed his index finger at Gregor as he was moving slowly forward. The violin fell silent. The middle lodger smiled, first shaking his head at his friends, and then looked down at Gregor once more. Rather than driving Gregor back, the father seemed to consider it more important for the time being to calm down the lodgers, although they were not at all upset and Gregor seemed to entertain them more than the violin recital. The father hurried over to them and with outstretched arms tried to push them into their own room and at the same time to block their view of Gregor with his own body. At this point they became really somewhat irritated, although one no longer knew whether that was because of the father's behaviour or because of the knowledge they had just acquired that they had, without being aware of it, a neighbour like Gregor. They demanded explanations from his father, raised their arms to make their points, tugged agitatedly at their beards, and moved back towards their room quite slowly. In the meantime, the isolation which had suddenly fallen upon his sister after the unexpected breaking off of the recital had overwhelmed her. She had held onto the violin and bow in her limp hands for a little while and had continued to look at the sheet music as if she was still playing. All at once she pulled herself together, placed the instrument in her mother's lap—the mother was still sitting in her chair having trouble breathing, for her lungs were labouring hard—and had run into the next room, which the lodgers, pressured by the father, were already approaching more rapidly. One could observe how under the sister's practised hands the covers and pillows on the beds were thrown high and then rearranged. Even before the lodgers had reached the room, she had finished fixing the beds and was slipping out. The father seemed once again so gripped by his stubbornness that he forgot about the respect which, after all, he must show his lodgers. He pressed on and on, until right in the door of the room the middle gentleman stamped loudly with his foot and thus brought the father to a standstill. "I hereby declare," the middle lodger said, raising his hand and casting his glance both on the mother and the sister, "that considering the disgraceful conditions prevailing in this apartment and family"— with this he spat decisively on the floor—"I immediately cancel my room. I will, of course, pay nothing at all for the days which I have lived here; on the contrary, I shall think about whether or not I will initiate some sort of action against you, something which—believe me—will be very easy to establish." He fell silent and looked directly in front of him, as if he was waiting for something. In fact, his two friends immediately joined in with their opinions, "We also give immediate notice." At that he seized the door handle and with a bang slammed the door shut.

The father groped his way tottering to his chair and let himself fall in it. It looked as if he was stretching out for his usual evening snooze, but the heavy nodding of his head, which appeared as if it had no support, showed that he was not sleeping at all. Gregor had lain motionless the entire time in the spot where the lodgers had caught him. Disappointment with the collapse of his plan and perhaps also weakness brought on by his severe hunger made it impossible for him to move. He was afraid and reasonably certain that they might launch a combined attack against him at any moment, and he waited. He was not even startled when the violin fell from the mother's lap, out from under her trembling fingers, and gave off a reverberating tone.

"My dear parents," said the sister banging her hand on the table by way of an introduction, "things cannot go on any longer in this way. Maybe if you don't understand that, well, I do. I will not utter my brother's name in front of this monster, and thus I say only that we must try to get rid of it. We have tried what is humanly possible to take care of it and to be patient. I believe that no one can criticize us in the slightest."

"She is right in a thousand ways," said the father to himself. The mother, who was still incapable of breathing properly, began to cough numbly with her hand held up over her mouth and a manic expression in her eyes.

The sister hurried over to her mother and held her forehead. The sister's words seemed to have led the father to certain reflections. He sat upright, played with his service hat among the plates, which still lay on the table from the lodgers' evening meal, and looked now and then at the motionless Gregor.

"We must try to get rid of it," the sister now said decisively to the father, for the mother, in her coughing fit, was not listening to anything. "It is killing you both. I see it coming. When people have to work as hard as we all do, they cannot also tolerate this endless torment at home. I just can't go on any more." And she broke out into such a crying fit that her tears flowed out down onto her mother's face. She wiped them off her mother with mechanical motions of her hands.

"Child," said the father sympathetically and with obvious appreciation, "then what should we do?"

The sister only shrugged her shoulders as a sign of the perplexity which, in contrast to her previous confidence, had now come over her while she was crying.

"If he understood us," said the father in a semi-questioning tone. The sister, in the midst of her sobbing, shook her hand energetically as a sign that there was no point thinking of that.

"If he understood us," repeated the father and by shutting his eyes he absorbed the sister's conviction of the impossibility of this point, "then perhaps some compromise would be possible with him. But as it is. . ."

"It has to go," cried the sister. "That is the only way, father. You must try to get rid of the idea that this is Gregor. The fact that we have believed this for so long, that is truly our real misfortune. But how can it be Gregor? If it were Gregor, he would have long ago realized that a communal life among human beings is not possible with such a creature and would have gone away voluntarily. Then we would not have a brother, but we could go on living and hon- our his memory. But this animal plagues us. It drives away the lodgers, will obviously take over the entire apartment, and leave us to spend the night in the lane. Just look, father," she suddenly cried out, "he's already starting up again." With a fright which was totally incomprehensible to Gregor, the sister even left the mo- ther, literally pushed herself away from her chair, as if she would sooner sacrifice her mother than remain in Gregor's vicinity, and rushed behind her father who, excited merely by her behaviour, also stood up and half raised his arms in front of the sister as though to protect her.

But Gregor did not have any notion of wishing to create problems for anyone and certainly not for his sister. He had just started to turn himself around in order to creep back into his room, quite a startling sight, since, as a result of his suffering condition, he had to guide himself through the difficulty of turning around with his head, in this process lifting and striking it against the floor several times. He paused and looked around. His good intentions seemed to have been recognized. The fright had lasted only for a moment. Now they looked at him in silence and sorrow. His mother lay in her chair, with her legs stretched out and pressed together, her eyes almost shut from weariness. The father and sister sat next to one another. The sister had put her hands around the father's neck.

"Now perhaps I can actually turn myself around," thought Gregor and began the task again. He couldn't stop puffing at the effort and had to rest now and then. Besides, no one was urging him on. It was all left to him on his own. When he had completed turning around, he immediately began to wander straight back. He was astonished at the great distance which separated him from his room and did not understand in the least how in his weakness he had covered the same distance a short time before, almost without noticing it. Always intent only on creeping along quickly, he hardly paid any attention to the fact that no word or cry from his family interrupted him. Only when he was already in the doorway did he turn his head, not completely, because he felt his neck growing stiff. At any rate, he still saw that behind him nothing had changed. Only the sister was standing up. His last glimpse brushed over the mother, who was now completely asleep.

He was only just inside his room when the door was pushed shut very quickly, bolted fast, and barred. Gregor was startled by the sudden commotion behind him, so much so that his little limbs bent double under him. It was his sister who had been in such a hurry. She was already standing up, had waited, and then sprung forward nimbly. Gregor had not heard anything of her approach. She cried out "Finally!" to her parents, as she turned the key in the lock.

"What now?" Gregor asked himself and looked around him in the darkness. He soon made the discovery that he could no longer move at all. He was not surprised at that. On the contrary, it struck him as unnatural that up to this point he had really been able up to move around with these thin little legs. Besides he felt relatively content. True, he had pains throughout his entire body, but it seemed to him that they were gradually becoming weaker and weaker and would finally go away completely. The rotten apple in his back and the inflamed surrounding area, entirely covered with white dust, he hardly noticed. He remembered his family with deep feelings of love. In this business, his own thought that he had to disappear was, if possible, even more decisive than his sister's. He remained in this state of empty and peaceful

reflection until the tower clock struck three in the morning. In front of the window he witnessed the beginning of the outside growing generally lighter. Then without willing it, his head sank all the way down, and from his nostrils his last breath flowed weakly out.

Early in the morning the cleaning woman came. In her sheer energy and haste she banged all the doors—in precisely the way people had already frequently asked her to avoid—so much so that once she arrived a quiet sleep was no longer possible anywhere in the entire apartment. In her customarily brief visit to Gregor she at first found nothing special. She thought he lay so immobile there on purpose and was playing the offended party. She gave him credit for as complete an understanding as possible. Since she happened to be holding the long broom in her hand, she tried to tickle Gregor with it from the door. When that was quite unsuccessful, she became irritated and poked Gregor a little, and only when she had shoved him from his place without any resistance did she become attentive. When she quickly realized the true state of affairs, her eyes grew large and she whistled to herself. However, she didn't restrain herself for long. She pulled open the door of the bedroom and yelled in a loud voice into the darkness, "Come and look. It's kicked the bucket. It's lying there. It's completely snuffed it!"

The Samsas sat upright in their marriage bed and had to get over their fright at the cleaning woman before they managed to grasp her message. But then Mr. and Mrs. Samsa climbed very quickly out of bed, one on either side. Mr. Samsa threw the bedspread over his shoulders, Mrs. Samsa came out only in her nightshirt, and like this they stepped into Gregor's room. Meanwhile, the door of the living room, in which Grete had slept since the lodgers had arrived on the scene, had also opened. She was fully clothed, as if she had not slept at all; her white face also seemed to indicate that. "Dead?" said Mrs. Samsa and looked questioningly at the cleaning woman, although she could have checked everything on her own and it was clear even without a check. "I should say so," said the cleaning woman and, by way of proof, poked Gregor's body with the broom a considerable distance more to the side. Mrs. Samsa made a movement, as if she wished to restrain the broom, but did not do it. "Well," said Mr. Samsa, "now we can give thanks to God." He crossed himself, and the three women followed his example. Grete, who did not take her eyes off the corpse, said, "Just look how thin he was. He has eaten nothing for such a long time. The meals which came in here came out again exactly the same." In fact, Gregor's body was completely flat and dry. That was apparent really for the first time, now that he was no longer raised on his small limbs and nothing else distracted one from looking.

"Grete, come into us for a moment," said Mrs. Samsa with a melancholy smile, and Grete went, not without looking back at the corpse, behind her parents into the bed room. The cleaning woman shut the door and opened the window wide. In spite of the early morning, the fresh air was partly tinged with warmth. It was already almost the end of March.

The three lodgers stepped out of their room and looked around for their breakfast, astonished that they had been forgotten. The middle one of the gentlemen asked the cleaning woman grumpily "Where is the breakfast?" However, she laid her finger to her lips and then quickly and silently indicated to the lodgers that they could come into Gregor's room. So they came and stood in the room, which was already quite bright, around Gregor's corpse, their hands in the pockets of their somewhat worn jackets.

Then the door of the bedroom opened, and Mr. Samsa appeared in his uniform, with his wife on one arm and his daughter on the other. All were a little tear stained. Now and then Grete pressed her face into her father's arm.

"Get out of my apartment immediately," said Mr. Samsa and ̄ted to the door, without letting go of the women. "What do ̄nean?" said the middle lodger, somewhat dismayed and with ̄ry smile. The two others kept their hands behind them and ̄tly rubbed them against each other, as if in joyful antici- ̄ ̄f a great squabble which must end up in their favour. "I mean exactly what I say," replied Mr. Samsa and went directly up to the lodger with his two female companions. The latter at first stood there motionless and looked at the floor, as if matters were arranging themselves in a new way in his head. "All right, then we'll go," he said and looked up at Mr. Samsa as if, suddenly overcome by humility, he was even asking fresh permission for this decision. Mr. Samsa merely nodded briefly and repeatedly to him with his eyes open wide. Following that, with long strides the lodger actually went out immediately into the hall. His two friends had already been listening for a while with their hands quite still, and now they hopped smartly after him, as if afraid that Mr. Samsa could step into the hall ahead of them and disturb their reunion with their leader. In the hall all three of them took their hats from the coat rack, pulled their canes from the umbrella stand, bowed silently, and left the apartment. In what turned out to be an entirely groundless mistrust, Mr. Samsa stepped with the two women out onto the landing, leaned against the railing, and looked over as the three lodgers slowly but steadily made their way down the long staircase, disappeared on each floor in a certain turn of the stairwell, and in a few seconds reappeared again. The further down they went, the more the Samsa family lost interest in them, and when a butcher with a tray on his head came up to meet them and then with a proud bearing ascended the stairs high above them, Mr. Samsa, together with the women, soon left the bannister, and they all returned, as if relieved, back into their apartment.

They decided to pass that day resting and going for a stroll. Not only had they earned this break from work, but there was no question that they really needed it. And so they sat down at the table and wrote three letters of apology: Mr. Samsa to his supervisor, Mrs. Samsa to her client, and Grete to her proprietor. During the writing the cleaning woman came in to say that she was going off, for her morning work was finished. The three people writing at first merely nodded, without glancing up. Only when the cleaning woman was still unwilling to depart, did they look up annoyed. "Well?" asked Mr. Samsa. The cleaning woman stood smiling in the doorway, as if she had a great stroke of luck to report to the family but would only do it if she was questioned thoroughly. The almost upright small ostrich feather in her hat, which had irritated Mr. Samsa during her entire service with them, swayed lightly in all directions. "All right then, what do you really want?" asked Mrs. Samsa, whom the cleaning lady respected more than the others. "Well," answered the cleaning woman, smiling so happily she couldn't go on speaking right away, "you mustn't worry about throwing out that rubbish from the next room. It's all taken care of." Mrs. Samsa and Grete bent down to their letters, as though they wanted to go on writing. Mr. Samsa, who noticed that the cleaning woman now wanted to start describing everything in detail, decisively prevented her with an outstretched hand. But since she was not allowed to explain, she remembered the great hurry she was in, and called out, clearly insulted, "Bye bye, everyone," then turned around furiously and left the apartment with a fearful slamming of the door.

"This evening she'll be given notice," said Mr. Samsa, but he got no answer from either his wife or from his daughter, because the cleaning woman seemed to have once again upset the tranquillity they had just attained. The women got up, went to the window, and remained there, with their arms about each other. Mr. Samsa turned around in his chair in their direction and observed them quietly for a while. Then he called out, "All right, come here then. Let's finally get rid of old things. And have a little consideration for me." The women attended to him at once. They rushed to him, caressed him, and quickly ended their letters.

Then all three left the apartment together, something they had not done for months now, and took the electric tram into the open air outside the city. The car in which they were sitting by themselves was totally engulfed by the warm sun. Leaning back comfortably in their seats, they talked to each other about future prospects, and they discovered that on closer observation these were not at all bad, for the three of them had employment, about which they had not really questioned each other at all, which was extremely favourable and with especially promising future prospects. The greatest improvement in their situation at this point, of course, had to come from a change of dwelling. Now they wanted to rent a smaller and cheaper apartment but better situated and generally more practical than the present one, which Gregor had chosen. While they amused themselves in this way, it struck Mr. and Mrs. Samsa, almost at the same moment, as they looked at their daughter, who was getting more animated all the time, how she had blossomed recently, in spite of all the troubles which had made her cheeks pale, into a beautiful and voluptuous young woman. Growing more silent and almost unconsciously understanding each other in their glances, they thought that the time was now at hand to seek out a good honest man for her. And it was something of a confirmation of their new dreams and good intentions when at the end of their journey their daughter stood up first and stretched her young body.

A NOTE ON THE TRANSLATOR

Ian Johnston is an emeritus professor at Vancouver Island University, Nanaimo, British Columbia, Canada. He is the author of *The Ironies of War: An Introduction to Homer's Iliad* and has translated a number of classic works into English, including the following (most of them published as books and ebooks by Richer Resources Publications).

Aeschylus, *Oresteia*
Aeschylus, *Persians*
Aeschylus, *Prometheus Bound*
Aeschylus, *Seven Against Thebes*
Aeschylus, *Suppliant Women*
Aristophanes, *Birds*
Aristophanes, *Clouds*
Aristophanes, *Frogs*
Aristophanes, *Knights*
Aristophanes, *Lysistrata*
Aristophanes, *Peace*
Cuvier, *Discourse on Revolutionary Upheavals on the Surface of the Earth*
Descartes, *Discourse on Method*
Descartes, *Meditations on First Philosophy*
Diderot, *D'Alembert's Dream and Rameau's Nephew*
Euripides, *Bacchae*
Euripides, *Electra*
Euripides, *Medea*
Euripides, *Orestes*
Homer, *Iliad*
Homer, *Odyssey*
Kafka, *Metamorphosis, A Hunger Artist, In the Penal Colony, and Other Stories*
Kant, *On Perpetual Peace*
Kant, *Universal History and Nature of the Heavens*
Lamarck, *Zoological Philosophy, Volume I*
Lucretius, *On the Nature of Things*
Nietzsche, *Birth of Tragedy*
Nietzsche, *Beyond Good and Evil*
Nietzsche, *Genealogy of Morals*
Nietzsche, *On the Uses and Abuses of History*
Ovid, *Metamorphoses*
Rousseau, *Discourse on the Sciences and the Arts*
Rousseau, *Discourse on the Origins of Inequality*
Rousseau, *Social Contract*
Sophocles, *Ajax*
Sophocles, *Antigone*
Sophocles, *Oedipus at Colonus*
Sophocles, *Oedipus the King*
Sophocles, *Philoctetes*

Ian Johnston has a web site (at http://records.viu.ca/~johnstoi/) where he has posted these translations, as well as a number of lectures, workbooks, essays, and book reviews.